MANDIE
AND THE
FORBIDDEN
ATTIC

Mandie Mysteries

1. *Mandie and the Secret Tunnel*
2. *Mandie and the Cherokee Legend*
3. *Mandie and the Ghost Bandits*
4. *Mandie and the Forbidden Attic*
5. *Mandie and the Trunk's Secret*
6. *Mandie and the Medicine Man*
7. *Mandie and the Charleston Phantom*
8. *Mandie and the Abandoned Mine*
9. *Mandie and the Hidden Treasure*
10. *Mandie and the Mysterious Bells*
11. *Mandie and the Holiday Surprise*
12. *Mandie and the Washington Nightmare*
13. *Mandie and the Midnight Journey*
14. *Mandie and the Shipboard Mystery*
15. *Mandie and the Foreign Spies*
16. *Mandie and the Silent Catacombs*
17. *Mandie and the Singing Chalet*
18. *Mandie and the Jumping Juniper*
19. *Mandie and the Mysterious Fisherman*
20. *Mandie and the Windmill's Message*
21. *Mandie and the Fiery Rescue*
22. *Mandie and the Angel's Secret*
23. *Mandie and the Dangerous Imposter*

Mandie's Cookbook

MANDIE
AND THE
FORBIDDEN
ATTIC

Lois Gladys Leppard

BETHANY HOUSE PUBLISHERS
MINNEAPOLIS, MINNESOTA 55438

Mandie and the Forbidden Attic
Lois Gladys Leppard

Library of Congress Catalog Card Number 84–72710

ISBN 0–87123–822–5

Published by Bethany House Publishers
A Ministry of Bethany Fellowship, Inc.
6820 Auto Club Road, Minneapolis, Minnesota 55438

Printed in the United States of America

To My Very Special Cousins,
H. D. "Jack" Wilson
and
Mary Ellen Mundy Wilson,

With Love and Thanks
for their
Encouragement Over the Years

About the Author

LOIS GLADYS LEPPARD has been a Federal Civil Service employee in various countries around the world. She makes her home in South Carolina.

The stories of her own mother's childhood are the basis for many of the incidents incorporated in this series.

Contents

Chapter 1 A Strange New School.............. 9

Chapter 2 Silly Lessons 20

Chapter 3 Mandie's Enemy................... 31

Chapter 4 Young Gentlemen Callers 40

Chapter 5 Locked Out in the Night 49

Chapter 6 April's Trouble.................... 56

Chapter 7 More Noises in the Night........... 65

Chapter 8 Caught! 75

Chapter 9 Visitors at Grandmother's House 86

Chapter 10 Snowball Disappears................ 96

Chapter 11 The Mystery Solved 106

Chapter 12 Grandmother to the Rescue......... 115

MANDIE'S TRAVELS

Cave

Little Tennessee River

Deep Creek

○ Uncle Ned's House

Cherokee Hospital
○

Bryson
City ○

Almond
Station
○

Tomahawk Trail

Bird-town

Cherokee
Reservation

Council
House
○

Asheville ○

Joe's
House ○

Buckner
Branch

Little Tennessee River

Charley
Gap ○

Tuckasegee River

Nantahala River

Wiggins Creek

Tomahawk Trail

Hightower
Gap

Ruby Mine ○

Franklin ○

North Carolina

Georgia

South Carolina

To
Charleston

Chapter 1 / A Strange New School

Mandie's heart did flipflops as the train came to a halt beside the depot in Asheville, North Carolina.

"Well, here we are," Uncle John said. "I see the rig from the school is out there."

Mandie could not speak. She knew the dreaded time for parting had come. She would be left at the school alone while her mother and Uncle John returned home to the city of Franklin where they lived. She couldn't stand the thought of leaving them.

It seemed like only yesterday that her father had died and she went to live with Uncle John. Mandie didn't know her real mother, Elizabeth, until Uncle John brought them together. Then before long Uncle John and Mandie's mother were married, and Mandie was delighted. But now, they were making her go to the boarding school her mother had attended.

"Come along, Amanda," her mother urged.

As though in a daze, Mandie trudged down the aisle. She felt numb and detached from the scene as she stepped off the train.

Elizabeth hurried over to the waiting surrey, and the old Negro driver came forward to greet her.

"Uncle Cal!" Elizabeth said as the family joined her. "This is my daughter, Amanda, and my husband, John Shaw."

Uncle Cal tipped his hat.

"John is my first husband's brother," she explained. "You probably remember Jim. I left the school to marry him. He was Amanda's father."

"Yessum, I sho' do 'member Mr. Shaw," the old man replied. "Pleased to meet you, Mr. John Shaw," he said, shaking hands.

Mandie held out her small gloved hand. "How do you do, Uncle Cal," she said.

"I'se jes' fine, Missy." The old man squeezed her hand warmly. "You sho' de spittin' image of yo' mama when she be 'bout yo' age," he said, surveying the little blue-eyed blonde. "Jes' wait 'til Phoebe see you. She gonna think Miz Lizbeth done come back to school agin."

Mandie smiled. "Thank you, Uncle Cal." Instantly, she knew she had a friend.

Uncle John began helping the old man load Mandie's trunk and bags onto the surrey. As Mandie watched them, pains of protest gripped her stomach. But she had promised her mother and Uncle John that she would give the school a try. They promised her that if she couldn't be happy there, they would bring her back home, and she could go to school in Franklin.

Mandie was determined to fight the sadness and loneliness of being separated from her mother and Uncle John. She would trust God to give her the strength.

As they drove the short distance from the train station to the school, Mandie rode in silence. She did not hear the horses clip-clopping down the cobblestone streets, nor her mother's conversation with Uncle Cal. She saw nothing of the town as they passed through. She was trying to be brave, but it wasn't easy.

As Uncle Cal turned the surrey up a half-circle graveled driveway, Mandie stared at the huge white clapboard house surrounded by magnolia trees at the top of a hill.

The surrey stopped in front of the long two-story porch supported by six huge white pillars. A small sign to the left of the heavy double doors read "The Misses Heathwood's School for Girls." Tall narrow windows trimmed with colorful stained glass flanked each side of the doors. Above the doors, matching stained glass edged a fan-shaped transom of glass panes.

Behind the bannisters along the veranda were white rocking chairs with green, flowered cushions. Over to the left, a wooden swing hung by chains attached to the ceiling. At the corner, the porch turned and went around the left side of the house.

Mandie's attention returned to the doorway as a short, thin, elderly lady, wearing a simple black dress, came out to welcome them. Leaving the surrey, John, Elizabeth and Mandie started across the lawn.

"My, my, Elizabeth, dear. I'm so glad to see you," the schoolmistress said, smoothing her jet black hair with her hand. "This must be your husband and Amanda, of course."

"Yes, Miss Prudence, this is my husband, John Shaw," Elizabeth replied.

John removed his hat and nodded his head slightly. "How do you do, ma'am," he said.

Miss Prudence nodded in acknowledgment.

"And, Amanda," Elizabeth continued, resting her neatly-gloved hand on Mandie's shoulder. She pushed her daughter a little forward. "Amanda, this is Miss Prudence Heathwood."

Not knowing what else to say, Mandie echoed her uncle's greeting. "How do you do, ma'am."

"Welcome, Amanda. I know you're going to like it here," Miss Prudence told her.

Mandie wished she could be that sure.

Miss Prudence called to the Negro who waited by the surrey. "Uncle Cal, please take Miss Amanda's things to the third floor, room three.

"Yessum," Uncle Cal replied.

Miss Prudence turned back to Elizabeth. "Do come in, Elizabeth—all of you," she said, leading the way.

They followed the woman through the doorway into a large center hallway. Mandie stared upward. Delicate plaster-of-Paris angels and roses decorated the high white ceiling. Across the hall a huge chandelier, which seemed to hold a hundred candles, hung near the curved staircase leading to a second-story balcony. Dark wooden wainscoting covered the lower third of the wallpapered walls.

Miss Prudence led them off to the right into an alcove furnished with huge tapestry-covered chairs. A large flower arrangement sat on a marble-topped table.

They sat down in big, comfortable chairs.

Elizabeth leaned forward. "John and I will be taking the train home this afternoon," she said.

"Oh? You aren't staying at your mother's?" Miss Prudence asked.

"No, she's out of town," Elizabeth answered.

She's always out of town when we come to Asheville, Mandie thought. *Maybe she is still angry with Uncle John for reuniting Mother and me after she went to so much trouble to separate us.*

Mandie hardly looked up when a maid came in to serve cold lemonade. Mandie's mother and Miss Prudence continued their conversation, but Mandie didn't hear it. She was deep in her own thoughts.

She still couldn't understand why her father hadn't revealed the truth about her mother and stepmother. Her stepmother had been so unkind. Without Uncle Ned, her father's old Cherokee friend, Mandie wouldn't have found her Uncle John and her real mother. *Maybe Grandmother doesn't want me because my father was half Cherokee*, she thought.

Suddenly Mandie realized that someone was talking to her. "I'm sorry, Mother, I didn't understand what you said," she apologized.

"Miss Prudence was saying that we may use the guest room on this floor to freshen up. It'll soon be time to go to the dining room," her mother explained.

Mandie quickly rose. "Yes, ma'am. That would be a good idea."

Miss Prudence led the way down the hallway. "Right this way," she said. "Of course, Elizabeth, you know where it is. I don't think we've changed a thing since you were a student here. We haven't even installed those new electric lights everyone is talking about."

She stopped at the guest-room doorway. "I'll meet you in the dining room at twelve sharp. The other girls have already arrived. We can accommodate only twenty at the table at a time, so we have two sittings."

"Then you have twice as many girls now as you did when I was here." Elizabeth smiled. "We'll be prompt."

The guest room was beautifully decorated. A handsome four-poster bed stood in the middle of the floor. Clean towels and a large ceramic bowl and pitcher of water waited on a washstand in the corner. But going to a door in the far wall by the fireplace, Elizabeth found a bathroom, complete with water tank high on the wall, and a chain to pull for flushing the commode. There was a bathtub standing on four feet that looked like claws, and an enormous marble lavatory with cut glass handles on the faucets.

"This is lovely. I should be out shortly," Elizabeth said, closing the bathroom door behind her.

Uncle John sat down in a velvet-covered chair near the bed. "I'll rest here," he said.

"Me too," Mandie added. Plopping down onto a foot-stool, she removed her bonnet and gloves, and discarded her small purse on the floor. She was wearing a very proper traveling dress of brown silk and matching buttoned shoes, white silk stockings under the long, full skirt, and white gloves with tiny pearl buttons. The outfit was only one of many that her mother had a seamstress make for Mandie's school term. Mandie was already tired of the fancy clothes. She sighed, propped her elbow on her knee, and rested her chin in her hand.

"Tired?" Uncle John asked.

"I'm so tired and disgusted already!" Mandie told him in a shaky voice. She fought back the tears.

"Come now, dear," he said, reaching to pat her blonde head. "You promised us you would at least try it."

"I know, Uncle John. It's just all so strange." She took a deep breath to steady her voice. "I've never been in a place like this before."

"It'll take time. But before you know it you'll be home for a holiday and telling us how much you like the school."

"I'll try. But please tell Uncle Ned not to forget his promise to visit me on the first full moon. That will be Thursday of next week."

"I will, Mandie. We all love that old Indian. I'm sure he'll keep his word to your father when he died to watch over you. He'll be here. You can depend on him."

The sound of laughter and talking drifted down the hall.

Uncle John looked at his pocket watch.

"Wash up, Mandie, and get your mother. It's time to eat."

A few minutes later, Elizabeth led the way to the huge dining room where several girls stood behind chairs around the long table. Sparkling red glass dishes lay on the crisp white tablecloth, ready for the meal. The Shaws hesitated just inside the French doors. Miss Prudence entered from the opposite side of the room and motioned for them to sit near her at the head of the table.

Mandie reluctantly took her place behind the chair next to Uncle John. On the other side of her, a tall girl with black hair and deep black eyes stared at her without speaking, or even smiling.

Miss Prudence shook a little silver bell as she stood at the head of the table. "Young ladies," she announced, "we will return our thanks." Miss Prudence watched to see that every head was bowed and then spoke, "Our Gracious Heavenly Father, we thank Thee for this food of which we are about to partake, and ask Thy blessings on it and on all who are present. Amen. Please be seated."

There was a scraping of chairs as they all sat down.

"Since everyone has arrived now," Miss Prudence continued, "we would like you to get acquainted. Please introduce yourselves and tell us where you are from. We will begin with Etrulia and go around the table."

The introductions began, but Mandie was too tense to remember the names.

Then the girl next to her spoke. "I'm April Snow," the black-haired girl said in a rebellious tone, "and I'm from Nashville, Tennessee."

There was silence and Mandie realized they were waiting for her to speak.

"My name is Amanda Shaw, Mandie for short, and I'm

from Franklin," she said, twisting her fingers together.

"And, young ladies," Miss Prudence added, "these are Amanda's parents, Mr. and Mrs. John Shaw."

John and Elizabeth smiled, but Mandie caught her breath. These were not her parents, plural. She had only one real parent—her mother. Miss Prudence knew that Uncle John was not Mandie's father. How could she say such a thing? Mandie wanted all the world to know that her dear father was Jim Shaw and that he was in heaven now. Mandie didn't dare speak up, but she realized it would be difficult to untangle Miss Prudence's remark.

At the end of the meal Miss Prudence stood again and rang the bell.

"Since classes don't begin until tomorrow," she announced, "you may have the rest of the day to unpack and get to know one another."

Everyone left quickly so that the table could be cleared and reset for the second seating. Miss Prudence took the opportunity to show the Shaws around.

On the main floor, they toured the dining room, kitchen, parlor, music room, library, and two classrooms. Miss Prudence's and Miss Hope's rooms were on this floor. A connecting room also served as the school office.

On the second floor, there were more classrooms, two huge bedrooms and two baths. Each bedroom had four double beds to accommodate eight girls. Mandie's room was on the third floor where the new students lived. There were three bedrooms with four double beds, two bathrooms, and more classrooms.

When they entered the last bedroom, Mandie was alarmed to find her trunk and bags standing at the foot of a huge bed.

"This is the room you will live in, Amanda," Miss Prudence informed her. "You will share this bed with April Snow, and there will be six others rooming with you."

Mandie cringed. *There's no privacy,* she thought, *not even to say my prayers!*

Minutes later, in the alcove downstairs, Mandie tearfully kissed her mother and Uncle John good-bye. Then Uncle Cal took them back to the train station.

Mandie sat alone in the alcove for a long time, trying to compose herself before encountering any of the other girls. She whispered a prayer asking God to see her mother and Uncle John safely home, and to give her the strength to live up to her mother's wishes.

Finally she slipped down the hall and into the guest bathroom to bathe her face. Still not wanting to talk to anyone, she went out onto the veranda and sat in the swing. But April Snow found her anyway.

Standing squarely in front of Mandie, she said, "I would suggest that you get busy and unpack your things, or do something with them. They are in the way. Everyone else has finished unpacking."

Mandie stood up quickly. "Oh, I'm sorry. I didn't stop to think—"

"There's no time to stop and think around here," April interrupted. She sauntered off to the other side of the porch.

Mandie took a deep breath to control her anger and headed for her new sleeping quarters. She met some of the girls coming down the stairs, and when she got to the bedroom she realized that the others had indeed finished.

At the evening meal everyone seemed to be talking to everyone else. No one spoke to Mandie. She silently pushed the food around on her plate until Miss Prudence rang the bell and stood to recite the rules.

"Young ladies," the schoolmistress began. "All lamps

will be extinguished at ten o'clock each night. No one is allowed out of the room after that. Aunt Phoebe, Uncle Cal's wife, will knock on your doors at seven in the morning to wake you. First breakfast sitting will be at seven-thirty. You are dismissed for the day now."

Mandie spent the evening by herself in a rocker at the end of the veranda. No one approached her for conversation, and she was glad to be left alone in her misery.

When bedtime came, April informed Mandie which side of the bed she could have and demanded that Mandie not wriggle around, snore, or talk in her sleep. Mandie numbly agreed and crawled into her side of the bed—next to the wall.

Unable to sleep, Mandie lay very still, not wanting to disturb April. She wondered what her mother and Uncle John were doing. She missed her friends back home. The girl next door, Polly Cornwallis, had been sent to a school in Nashville. Mandie wondered if Polly liked her school. *I can't wait until next week*, she thought. *Then Uncle Ned will be here*. He truly cared about her. And he would give her a report on her other Indian friends and relatives. She hoped he would also have news from her special friend, Joe, Dr. Woodard's son.

Mandie turned her head on the pillow. She was worried about her kitten, Snowball, too. She had never left him before.

After what seemed like hours, Mandie could hear the girls' slow, even breathing around the room, and she decided that everyone else was asleep. Slowly and quietly, she crept out of the end of the bed. She slipped out into the hallway, barefooted and in her nightgown. She remembered seeing a window seat at the other end of the hall. On tiptoe she made her way there where she could sit, and look at the stars, and talk to God.

There was not one minute of privacy in this place.

Near the window seat Mandie noticed a small bedroom with only one bed. The room was right next to the stairs to the attic and the servants' stairway going down. Mandie wished she could have that room.

She thought of when she lived with her father and step-mother on the farm at Charley Gap. Everything was fine until her father died and her stepmother quickly remarried. She couldn't get rid of Mandie soon enough. Uncle Ned had helped her find her Uncle John. She didn't even know about him until then. Mandie remembered the first time she met her mother. And then when Uncle John and her mother married, Mandie was excited to be part of a real family again.

Suddenly Mandie heard a sound of metal clanging and boards squeaking. The noise seemed to be coming from the attic above her. She froze, holding her breath and listening. But nothing else happened.

Maybe one of the servants sleeps in an attic room, she thought. But then she remembered that Miss Prudence had said Uncle Cal and Aunt Phoebe had their own little cottage in the backyard. The other servants lived in town and came in during the day. *Oh, well, maybe it was a rat.* She took a deep breath, trying to dismiss her concern.

There! It did it again! The same noise. It couldn't be a rat. Mandie wasn't going to wait to hear the noise again. She ran quietly back to her room.

Slipping into bed she lay awake, listening. Would she hear the noise again, or was her room too far away? The only sound was the deep breathing of the other girls.

With her thoughts still on the noise, she finally drifted off to sleep. Someday she would have to sneak up to the attic and investigate.

Chapter 2 / Silly Lessons

The next morning, Mandie dressed and appeared for breakfast. The other girls ignored her, but Mandie was content to be left alone.

The morning was spent in the classrooms with two young lady teachers who lived in town. When Mandie heard about the so-called social graces the girls were expected to learn, she silently rebelled.

"Each girl will practice walking up and down the hallway, balancing a book on her head," Miss Cameron instructed. "This will correct your posture and develop that dainty step that all ladies have."

The girls laughed.

Miss Cameron tapped her pencil on her desk. "That is not conduct becoming to a lady. You will show proper courtesy toward adults," she said sternly. "And I assure you that carrying a book on your head without its falling is not easy, however frivolous it may sound."

At first Mandie thought the task was impossible. Then she learned to go very slowly and hold her breath.

The next lesson was how to stoop properly to pick up something from the floor.

"A lady never bends forward with her posterior in the

20

air," Miss Cameron informed them. "You must always bend your knees and slowly lower your body until your hand can reach the desired object. Then you slowly straighten up, smoothing your skirts as you stand."

This exercise made Mandie feel like an old lady too feeble to bend.

And then Miss Cameron offered instructions on how a lady controls her voice. "A lady never, never shouts," she said. "Even when she is angry, she keeps her voice under control. A lady never talks loudly to someone too far away to hear normal conversation. She walks over to the person to talk to them, rather than yelling from a distance."

Such silly stuff, Mandie thought. She was thoroughly disgusted with the school. *How could I ever endure it without God's help?* she wondered.

At the noon meal Miss Prudence introduced a new girl who had just arrived. She sat on the other side of Mandie.

"Young ladies, this is Celia Hamilton from Richmond," Miss Prudence told them. "She will occupy the small vacant room on the third floor."

Mandie turned to the tall, slender girl with thick, curly auburn hair and looked into the saddest eyes she had ever seen.

Mandie's heart went out to her. She smiled and said, "Welcome."

"Thank you," Celia answered with a faraway look in her green eyes.

Neither said anything more, and when Miss Prudence dismissed them after the meal, Mandie had to go on to the next class on her list.

Celia didn't show up for supper. Miss Prudence announced that the new girl was tired from her trip and was excused from the evening meal so that she could retire early.

After the dining room had been cleared, Mandie and the others went out onto the veranda. Mandie sat alone while the other girls talked in small groups. After a while, Mandie went to the kitchen to get a drink of water.

As she pushed open the swinging door, Mandie almost collided with an old Negro woman who was tidying up the kitchen.

"I'm sorry," she quickly apologized.

The woman stopped working and stared at her. "Lawsy mercy, if you ain't Miz Lizbeth all over agin."

Mandie smiled and held out her hand.

"You must be Aunt Phoebe, Uncle Cal's wife. He said you'd say that when you saw me." Mandie giggled. "I'm Amanda Shaw, Elizabeth Shaw's daughter. They call me Mandie."

"And why ain't dat man tole me Miz Lizbeth's got a daughter and dat she be right heah under my nose." Aunt Phoebe put her arm around the girl and gave her a big squeeze. "Lawsy mercy, Missy Manda. I sho' am proud to have you heah."

"I'm not so glad to be here, Aunt Phoebe," Mandie confided.

"Heah, lemme git you a glass of dis heah milk I'se puttin' 'way and you set right down theah and tell old Phoebe what be wrong."

The woman quickly poured a glass of milk from the pitcher on the sideboard and handed it to Mandie. She motioned to the table in the corner. They sat down, and soon Mandie was opening her heart to Aunt Phoebe and telling her all her troubles.

"So, you see, Aunt Phoebe, I really don't want to be here," Mandie admitted. "I think it's a prissy school. I don't care about learning all those silly things they've been teaching us today. I'm not that kind of person. I love to live the way God intended we should—walk, chase butterflies, watch birds, and maybe even climb trees," she added with a big grin.

"Missy Manda, you sho' not like yo' mother when she yo' age. She liked to dress up and act like a lady."

"But my mother was brought up that way. I wasn't. I lived in the mountains in a log cabin almost all my life, and my friends are not society people. Why, my best friends are Indians and country people who would make fun of these put-on airs." Mandie whirled the empty glass on the table.

"But now you live wid yo' mother. You got to live de way she do," Aunt Phoebe reminded her. "Her pa was a rich man. And now she be married to Mistuh John Shaw. He be de richest man dis side o' Richmon'."

Mandie laughed. "That's exactly what Liza said about Uncle John."

"And who be Liza?"

"Liza is my friend. She works at Uncle John's house in Franklin." Mandie smiled. "She's always getting into trouble with Aunt Lou. Aunt Lou is the boss. She runs the house for Uncle John."

"Dey be my kind o' people? Dark skinned?"

"Yes, Aunt Phoebe. Why, you even remind me of Aunt Lou, except that she is much fatter," Mandie teased.

"Well, you say Aunt Lou be de boss theah, den I be de boss heah," the old woman said, rising from the table. "It be time fo' you to go to yo' room. It soon be ten o'clock and you don't wanta git in bad wid Miz Prudence, leastways not whilst you still new."

"I didn't realize it was so late." Mandie quickly embraced the old woman. "Good night. I'll see you tomorrow."

"Young ladies not 'llowed in de kitchen, and I don't go in de dinin' room. I does de cookin'. Millie does de waitin' on de table."

"But you have a house in the backyard, don't you? I'll come back there to visit you."

"I don' know 'bout dat. Ain't nobody ever done dat 'fore. It might not be 'llowed."

"Well, I won't ask." Mandie grinned. "I'll see you as soon as I can find a chance."

Hurrying up the stairs to her room, Mandie found the other girls in their nightgowns, talking or reading in bed. April lay reading, propped up with both pillows. She looked up. Mandie quickly entered the room, took her nightgown from her designated drawer in the huge bureau, and ran for the bathroom to undress.

When Mandie returned in her nightgown, carrying her clothes, April looked up again.

"What's the matter? You afraid to undress in front of the other girls?" April asked.

"Of course not," Mandie replied, hanging her dress on the hook assigned to her. "I took a quick bath."

"Bath? You have to get a time on the schedule to do that. The rest of us have already made up a list," April informed her.

"A list?" Mandie went to the side of the bed to get in. "What do you mean?"

"With eight girls to a bathroom, we had to decide who was going to take a bath when. So, four of us will be taking baths at night and four in the morning," April explained. "Each girl will have just ten minutes in the bathroom. The only ten minutes left is from six-twenty to six-thirty in the morning. No one wanted to get up that early." April grinned. "And since you weren't here when we made up the schedule, you'll have to take your bath then."

Silence fell over the room. The other girls watched for Mandie's reaction.

"That's fine with me." Mandie gave a little laugh as she slid between the sheets. "I like to get up early. I've been doing that all my life."

"You'll get tired of it," April said.

Mandie reached for a pillow behind April and gave it a yank. "I believe you have my pillow. There's only one pillow for each girl."

April pressed backward, trying to prevent her from pulling it away, but Mandie succeeded. She plumped up the pillow and lay down.

"Humph!" April said, rearranging the pillow that was left.

Suddenly a loud bell rang from somewhere nearby. The girls looked startled. Mandie sat up in bed.

April laughed. "That's the huge bell in the backyard. It's ten o'clock. They want to be sure we know it." She stuck the book she was reading under the mattress and blew out the oil lamp by the bed. The other girls quickly extinguished their lights, and the room became dark.

Mandie lay very still, not wishing to disturb the haughty girl sharing her bed. But the other girls continued whispering and giggling.

After a while April raised her voice to them. "All right, maybe you aren't sleepy but I am, and I want quiet in this room," she ordered. "Remember, they will wake us up at the ungodly hour of seven o'clock and those taking morning baths have to be up before that. So stop the noise and go to sleep," she commanded.

Although they quit talking immediately, for a long time there was the sound of restless tossing and turning in the other beds. Finally April dozed off and soon the only sound was the quiet breathing of the sleeping girls.

Mandie was not sleepy, and she hadn't had a chance to say her prayers, so she slipped out of bed and walked softly to the window seat at the end of the hall.

As she sat there looking at the moonlight among the trees and the stars twinkling in the sky, she heard a muffled sob. Tiptoeing to the stairway leading to the attic, she stopped and listened. No, it wasn't coming from the attic. It must be in the small bedroom. She eased up to the door and listened. Someone was definitely crying. She couldn't decide whether to open the door or not. Then she remembered the new girl, Celia. She was in that room because the other rooms were all full.

Mandie turned the doorknob and pushed the door slightly. In the dim moonlight from the windows she could see a sobbing figure on the bed. She stepped inside and softly shut the door behind her.

"Celia, is that you?" she whispered loudly.

The sobs immediately stopped, and Celia turned to see who was in her room.

"Celia, it's Mandie. What's wrong?" she asked, approaching the bed.

The other girl sat up. "Oh, they'll catch you out of your room!" she cried in a shaky voice.

Mandie sat on the side of the bed. "Everyone else is asleep," she said. "Now tell me what's wrong."

"Oh, Mandie, I'm just lonely and—and—" She began to sob.

"I'm lonely, too," Mandie replied. "But there's something else wrong, isn't there?"

"Y-Yes," the girl sobbed, pushing the pillows up against the headboard.

"What is it, Celia? Tell me. Maybe I can help."

"No one can bring my father back," Celia cried.

"Your father? He's dead?"

"That's why I was late coming to school," Celia explained.

"He died recently?"

"He—he was thrown from a horse last week. He was just—just buried the day before yesterday. Oh, Mandie, I loved him so much!"

Tears came into Mandie's blue eyes. She put her hand on the other girl's shoulder. "I know how you feel. My father . . . died, too. And I loved him very much. I miss him, and I think about him every day, remembering all the wonderful times we had together."

Celia dried her eyes. "Did he die suddenly?"

"Yes, he wasn't sick very long," Mandie told her. "I know how you feel, Celia. I loved my father more than anyone else on this earth. But, you know, he's up there in heaven now, waiting for me. Someday I'll be with him again."

"Do you really believe that, Mandie?"

"Believe it? Of course I believe it. Please don't tell me you don't."

"I know it's all in the Bible, and I go to church and pray, but it's so hard to give him up." She broke into sobs again.

Mandie put her arm around the shaking girl. "Celia, please don't cry. It won't help at all. I know because I've been through it. You just have to throw your shoulders back, hold your head high, and believe in God," she said. "Celia, you have a mother, don't you?"

"Yes, my mother couldn't bring me to school. She was deep in shock over my father's death. I didn't want to leave her like that, but she made me come."

"She was probably right. I think it would be better to be here with other girls—to keep occupied. When I lost my father I didn't have anyone to turn to. My stepmother, who I thought was my real mother, got married again right after my father went to heaven. She sent me away to work for another family. If it hadn't been for Uncle Ned, I wouldn't have had anyone to talk to."

"Who is Uncle Ned? And how did you get here if you were sent away to work?"

"Celia, you wouldn't believe what happened to me. You see, Uncle Ned promised my father that he would watch over me when he died. Uncle Ned is a very old Indian, and he really keeps his promise to my father. He helped me find my father's brother." Mandie took a quick breath. "I didn't even know my father had a brother. And when I found Uncle John, he got in touch with my real mother and got us together. And then he married my mother."

"That's quite a story, Mandie, but I think I get it. Do you really have an Indian friend?"

"Sure, lots of them. In fact, my father's mother was a full-blooded Cherokee."

"Oh, Mandie! It doesn't make any difference to me, but if I were you I wouldn't tell that to the other girls in this school. They're all so uppity they would probably give you a rough time about it."

"I don't care if they know. I'm proud of my Indian blood. But since they haven't tried to make friends with me, I won't volunteer the information. Everyone seems to know everyone else, but I don't know anyone." Mandie sighed. "I didn't want to come to this silly school anyway."

"But, Mandie, you know me. I'm your friend."

"Thank you, Celia. I liked you from the minute I saw you. You didn't put on airs like the other girls."

Celia smiled. Mandie was glad to be able to take her friend's mind off her sadness.

Suddenly they heard the noise that Mandie had heard the night before. The sound of metal clanging and boards squeaking seemed to come from the attic. The two girls froze. The dimness of the room made it all the more eerie.

"Did you hear that?" Celia whispered.

"Yes, and I heard it last night, too. It sounds like something in the attic."

The noise stopped. The girls remained still, waiting for it to begin again. But it didn't.

"I don't like being way down here in this room alone," Celia told her.

"Maybe I could move in here with you," Mandie offered. "I sure wouldn't mind getting away from April."

"Would you want to, really?"

"I'd love to. Let's ask Miss Prudence tomorrow."

"Yes, let's do."

"If I move in here, maybe we could investigate the attic together, and find out what's making that noise."

"You mean actually go up there?" Celia stared at her with her mouth open.

"Sure. We could sneak out after everyone else is asleep," Mandie said. "You're not afraid to go up there, are you?"

"No, no, no. But what if we got caught?"

"Nobody's going to catch us. This room is far away from the others, and we'll be real quiet."

"But there's no telling what's up there."

"If we find anything awful we can scream our heads off. We'd get caught, but at least someone would rescue us." Mandie got up and started for the door. "Right now, though, I'd better get back to my bed before someone misses me."

"But I'm afraid to be left alone, especially with those noises up there."

Mandie reached for the doorknob and her hand touched a key sticking out. "Hey, there's a key in the door. As soon as I leave, you lock the door. Then no one can come in and bother you."

Celia jumped up and hurried over to examine the key.

"Thank goodness!" she exclaimed.

"I'll catch up with you tomorrow, and we can ask Miss Prudence if I can move in here with you," Mandie told her. "Now lock the door. Good night."

Mandie softly opened the door and stepped out into the hall. Hearing the lock click behind her, she hurried down the hallway and slipped back into her own bed. She hoped she could persuade Miss Prudence to let her move in with Celia. Then the two of them could find out what that noise was.

Chapter 3 / Mandie's Enemy

Mandie and Celia met outside the dining room at breakfast and stopped to talk.

"Did you hear anything else last night?" Mandie whispered.

Celia shook her auburn curls. "Not a sound. I locked my door and went to sleep right away. Are we still going to ask Miss Prudence if you can move in with me?"

"Oh, yes—that is, if you want me to."

"Please do, Mandie. I'm afraid to be alone in that room. It's so isolated."

Miss Prudence came up behind them and Mandie turned around.

"May Celia and I speak to you for a few minutes after we eat?"

The schoolmistress looked from one girl to the other. "Of course, Amanda. I'll see you in my office."

Miss Prudence stepped into the dining room and stood at the head of the table. The girls took their places behind their chairs. Mandie and Celia smiled at each other.

The schoolmistress kept glancing at Mandie and Celia during the entire meal, as if wondering what they wanted to talk about. Mandie had not made friends with the other girls, and Celia seemed to be living in a world all her own. Aware of Celia's sad circumstances, Miss Prudence had placed the girls together at the table, hoping they would develop a friendship.

After the meal, the two girls hurried out of the dining room, getting to the office ahead of Miss Prudence. They waited in the hallway.

The assistant schoolmistress, Miss Hope, was just leaving the office. She supervised the second sitting in the dining room.

"Did you girls want something?" she asked.

"We're waiting for Miss Prudence," Mandie told her.

Miss Prudence hurried toward them down the hallway.

"Well, here she is now," Miss Hope said. "Oh, dear, I almost forgot to take my announcements with me." She turned back into the office.

Miss Hope was shifting papers on the nearby desk when her sister, Miss Prudence, invited the girls into the office.

"Now," Miss Prudence began, "sit down and tell me what you wanted to see me about." The girls sat down in the armchairs in front of the desk.

Mandie looked at her friend and then at Miss Hope. Celia seemed frightened of the old schoolmistresses. Miss Hope appeared preoccupied with hunting for her papers.

Mandie took a deep breath. "I would like permission to move into Celia's room with her," she began. "She's all alone and so far away from the others."

Miss Prudence looked from one girl to the other. "It's not our policy to shift girls around once they are settled in a room," she began. "It would create quite a commotion if everyone requested to move."

"But I'm afraid to stay by myself in that room," Celia ventured. "Last night I just happened to find the key in the lock and I locked the door."

"No doors are to be locked. You may bring me the key at supper," Miss Prudence replied. "This place is new to you. You will get used to it after a while. Now, if that is all you two wanted, I have other things to do."

Miss Hope stood at the door, listening.

Mandie looked at her friend and began to protest. "But, Miss Prudence, Celia and I have so much in common."

"What Mandie means," Celia said, "is that we have both lost our fathers. She came to talk to me last night when she heard me crying."

The schoolmistress bristled. "She went to your room? What time was this?"

Mandie decided there was no point in lying. Celia had unintentionally given her away. "It was after ten o'clock," Mandie admitted. "I couldn't sleep, and I walked down the hallway. I heard Celia crying, so I went into her room to see if I could do anything. As we talked we found out we had both lost our fathers," Mandie explained.

"Young lady," Miss Prudence said sternly, "you know that it is against the rules to go outside your room after ten o'clock at night, much less visit in another room. Did you not hear me recite the rules yesterday?"

The two girls trembled at hearing her firm tone.

"Miss Prudence, I'm sorry I—" Mandie apologized.

"Sister," Miss Hope interrupted, "I see no harm in what Amanda has done. Quite the contrary. One of us should have checked on Celia to see that she was all right. We knew about her father's tragedy."

"Sister, I am handling this matter," Miss Prudence cut her short. "Now you two will obey rules here without any exceptions. Is that understood?"

"Yes, ma'am," Celia meekly replied.

"Yes, Miss Prudence," Mandie echoed. "I'm sorry I broke the rules, but Celia was all by herself in that room, and she was terribly sad and lonely. Could I please move in with her? Please?"

Miss Prudence looked at her sharply. Amanda didn't give up easily.

Neither did Miss Hope. "Sister, I see no harm in allowing Amanda to move into the room with Celia," she said. "In fact, I think it would be a good idea. That room is too isolated for one girl alone. Of course, I know you are handling the matter, but that is my opinion."

Miss Prudence was silent for a long moment, looking from her sister to the two girls. Mandie and Celia held their breath, waiting.

Concern clouded Miss Prudence's eyes. "And suppose some of the other girls hear about this and decide they want to move around also?" she asked her sister.

"Let's say there has to be a good reason to move. In this case I think we have a very good reason," Miss Hope replied. "And if there should be a good reason for some other girl to move, then we will allow that, too."

Miss Prudence cleared her throat before speaking. "All right, Sister, if you want to be held responsible for any other requests to move, then we will get Uncle Cal to move Amanda's things into the room with Celia," Miss Prudence agreed. She looked at the girls sternly, "And you two young ladies, just remember this. There will be no more violations of the school rules. Next time, Amanda, it will be much more serious."

"Yes, ma'am. Thank you, Miss Prudence," Mandie replied.

Celia added her thanks, and the girls smiled at Miss Hope.

Miss Hope left the office quickly with her papers in her

hand. "I almost forgot it's time for me to go to the dining room," she said.

That afternoon, while the other students spent their free period on the veranda, Mandie and Celia helped Uncle Cal move Mandie's belongings.

The two girls, with their arms full of clothes, followed Uncle Cal out of Mandie's old room and walked straight into April's path.

"So, you just can't take it, huh?" April said, blocking their way. "I know the other girls have told you that my mother is a Yankee and my grandfather was a Union soldier, but I didn't think you would move out on account of that."

Mandie frowned. "But I didn't know that, April," she protested. "Besides, that doesn't make any difference to me, none at all."

"I don't believe you. Why else would you move out?"

"Really, April, I didn't know anything at all about you," Mandie insisted. "And what difference does it make which side your family was on? The War of Northern Aggression has been over for many, many years now."

"Mandie is moving into my room because I was afraid to stay there by myself," Celia told her.

"Afraid, huh?" April scoffed. "What're you afraid of?"

Mandie pushed past April. "Oh, come on, Celia. We don't have time to waste."

"You'll be sorry," April called as the two hurried down the hallway.

"I see now why you wanted to get away from that girl," Celia whispered.

Mandie soon realized another advantage of staying in the isolated room. The time would soon arrive for Uncle Ned to visit her, and it would be much easier to slip out of this room to meet him.

On the night of the full moon, the two girls sat talking in the dark, waiting for everyone else to go to sleep. Mandie couldn't wait to meet Uncle Ned in the yard. The ten o'clock bell had already rung and all the lamps were out.

Mandie told Celia her plan. "As soon as I get down the steps and into the yard, I'll come around to where I can watch this window. If you hear anyone coming, just close the window. I'll hurry back in," she said.

"I'll keep watch, Mandie, but I want to meet Uncle Ned."

"If he sees anyone besides me, he'll leave. Maybe the next time he comes you can meet him."

"Please ask him. Don't forget," Celia begged.

Mandie, still dressed, picked up a dark shawl to put over her head so that her blonde hair wouldn't shine in the moonlight.

"I won't forget." She crept out into the hallway. She had already planned her way out of the house in preparation for Uncle Ned's visit.

Hurrying down the servants' stairway in the dark, she ended up in the kitchen. The moon shone through the windows, so she could see the bolt on the outside door. Sliding the bolt over, she opened the door. Outside, she kept close to the shrubbery around the house and made her way to the side yard. She glanced up at the open window. Everything was all right so far.

Mandie didn't know where Uncle Ned would wait for her. Cautiously, she stepped out into the open, hoping he would see her and come on out. Her heart beat wildly, and she kept turning to watch for him. As she waited, her hopes began to fade. She was afraid he would forget to come or that circumstances beyond his control might prevent his visit.

Then she heard his familiar bird whistle nearby. She

turned to see him standing in the shadows of a huge magnolia tree. She ran and threw her arms around him. Tears of joy streamed down her cheeks.

"Uncle Ned! Uncle Ned! I knew you would come!" she cried as he embraced her.

"Sit, Papoose," he said, pointing to a white bench by the walkway. "Must hurry. Not want someone see Papoose. Make trouble."

They sat down and Mandie held his old, wrinkled hand.

"Oh, I'm so glad to see you," she said. "This is a miserable place, Uncle Ned, and they expect you to learn such silly things!"

"But Papoose must get book learning. I promise Jim Shaw," the old man replied. "Everything in this earth life not happy. Must do unhappy things, too."

"I know. I'll have to stay here and learn all these silly things. But how I wish I were home and could see all my friends. How is everybody?" she asked.

"All friends fine," he said with a smile. "Send much love." Uncle Ned looked at her closely. "Papoose make friends here?"

"I have one good friend. Celia Hamilton. She's my roommate. The other girls are too snobbish," Mandie told him. "Celia is keeping watch for me in that window right up there." She pointed. "She will let me know if anyone comes. Uncle Ned, she wants to meet you."

"Next time, Papoose." The old man stood up, pulled an envelope out of his belt, and handed it to Mandie. "Friends write Papoose letters."

Mandie gave a muffled squeal. "Oh, thank you!" She felt the envelope. *It must have quite a few letters in it*, she thought.

The old man looked toward the sky. "Must go now," he

said. "I ask Big God watch over Papoose." He squeezed her small hand, then leaned over to embrace her.

"Thank you, Uncle Ned. And I'll ask God to watch over you and all my friends until I can return. Please come back as soon as you can. Please!"

"Next time moon changes I come," he told her. "Go back in house now. I watch."

Mandie kissed his wrinkled cheek and ran for the back door. At the doorway she stopped and waved good-bye. Even though she couldn't see him in the darkness, she knew he was watching.

Inside the kitchen she carefully wrapped the shawl around the envelope. Then she went to the sink and got a drink of water.

The narrow servants' stairs were so dark Mandie couldn't see April blocking the way. Caught up in her thoughts, Mandie almost ran into her.

"Well, well, well! Where have you been?" April asked.

Mandie jumped. "I got a drink of water in the kitchen," she said quickly. She hoped April wouldn't see the shawl she held behind her.

"And what's wrong with the water in our bathroom upstairs?"

"I don't drink water out of bathrooms," Mandie said, imitating the snobbish tone of some of the other girls. "Now move out of my way, or I'll scream and the whole school will come running."

"You wouldn't dare!"

"Just stand there and see." Mandie tried to nudge her aside.

April stared at her a moment and then moved slightly.

"All right, you get through this time, but just remember, I know you were out of your room well after ten o'clock."

"And so were you," Mandie taunted, running up the stairs.

Celia was waiting at the door. "Is everything all right?"

"Fine, except I met April Snow as I was coming up the stairs. I have an idea she'll try to cause trouble," Mandie said. "But look!" She held up the envelope in the dim light. "Uncle Ned brought me letters from everybody."

Mandie draped her shawl over the back of a chair and sat down in the moonlight by the window. She tore open the envelope and excitedly shared her letters with her friend. Everyone was well, and everyone hoped Mandie was enjoying the school. They all said they missed her and hoped she'd soon come home, at least for a visit.

But April wasn't through with Mandie.

Chapter 4 / Young Gentlemen Callers

The next morning, Mandie's shawl was missing. She had hung it across the back of a chair while she read her letters, but now it wasn't there! Both girls looked all around the room, but they couldn't find it anywhere.

"Thank goodness I put my letters under my pillow!" Mandie exclaimed. "Otherwise they might have disappeared, too."

"Do you think April took your shawl?" Celia asked.

"I don't know. I can't imagine why she would do a thing like that. I sure wish Miss Prudence hadn't made us give her our key."

"Are you going to tell Miss Prudence about the shawl?"

"Not yet. Maybe whoever took it will bring it back," Mandie replied.

After making their bed, the girls laid their nightgowns across the foot of the bed, according to the school rule, and went downstairs.

Later, the girls didn't have time to think about the shawl. The students from Mr. Chadwick's School for Boys came across town to call on all the new girls for afternoon tea.

Miss Prudence told them it would be an opportunity for them to practice their social graces. "You will be graded on how you conduct yourselves," she reminded them.

Mandie wore her pale blue voile dress with white sprigs

of baby's breath scattered among its folds. Around her neck, she clasped the strand of tiny pearls Uncle John had given her as a going away present. She let her blonde curls hang free around her shoulders.

Celia sat beside her friend in the parlor, dressed in a bright green muslin dress with a matching hair ribbon. She twisted her handkerchief and blushed at even the thought of a boy speaking to her. She wanted to hide in a corner by herself.

"You stay right here with me, Celia," Mandie told her. "We need each other's support. This is just something we have to do."

"But Miss Prudence said each boy had drawn one of our names. There's no telling what kind of boys we'll end up with," Celia protested.

"If we don't like them, we just won't talk," Mandie said.

The girls heard the sound of horses outside, and in a few minutes Miss Prudence entered the parlor with a tall, thin man wearing spectacles.

"Young ladies, this is Mr. Chadwick," she told the girls. "His young men have arrived. Now, when they appear at the doorway and call your name, please rise and go outside. We will serve tea on the veranda as soon as all names have been called. Now, Mr. Chadwick, I believe we're ready."

"Thank you, Miss Heathwood," the man answered. "Excuse me, ladies." Stepping back to the doorway, he beckoned to the first boy in line in the hall.

The boy stood in the doorway, introduced himself as William Massey, and called, "Miss Etrulia Batson."

Etrulia, shy and quiet, stood up shakily. "I'm Etrulia Batson," she said.

William stepped forward, offered her his arm, and escorted her out of the parlor.

The line continued. Mandie and Celia clutched each other's hands as the tension mounted.

A boy of medium height, with a shy smile and unruly brown curls, stepped to the doorway. "I'm Robert Rogers, and I'm looking for Miss Celia Hamilton," he announced.

Mandie nudged her friend, but Celia froze. "Get up," Mandie whispered. "He called your name. Isn't he cute?"

Celia managed to get to her feet. She nervously smoothed the folds of her long skirt and took a deep breath. In a soft voice she replied, "I'm Celia Hamilton."

Robert strode forward, smiling. "I was afraid of what I'd get, and here I got the prettiest girl in the school," he told her.

Celia blushed. As they left the room, she saw Mandie smile at her.

With the line dwindling, Mandie began to think that maybe they would run out of boys, and she wouldn't have to bother being nice to someone. But the very last boy in line was hers.

A tall, handsome young lad with brown hair and dark brown eyes stepped to the doorway. Seeing Mandie was the only girl left in the room, he laughed.

"My name is Thomas Patton and I'm looking for Miss Amanda Shaw," he said, bowing slightly. "This was worth waiting for."

Mandie rose, straightened her skirts, and lifted her chin. "I'm Amanda Shaw," she replied. Then with a nervous giggle she added, "My friends call me Mandie, but they don't like nicknames at this school."

"My friends call me Tommy," the boy whispered loudly, "but nicknames aren't permitted at our school either. They want us to learn how to be real gentlemen, and they say real gentlemen don't go by nicknames." He offered his arm and Mandie tucked her hand in the crook of his elbow. "Just between you and me, I don't think they'll ever make a real gentleman out of me."

Mandie laughed as they went out onto the veranda. "And I know they won't ever make a real lady out of me. It's impossible."

The other girls turned to look as Mandie and Tommy sat down near April and her escort. Mandie looked around for Celia, and saw her at the other end of the porch. She was listening attentively to her new friend.

"Where are you from, Mandie?" Tommy asked.

"Franklin, North Carolina," she replied. "And you?"

"I'm from Charleston, South Carolina," he said.

Mandie's eyes widened. "Charleston? Where the beaches are? I've never seen the ocean. Tell me about it, please. What is it like?"

"It's the biggest body of water I have ever seen," he teased. Then more seriously he added, "You know that already, of course. But when the tide comes in, it brings huge waves that splash water way up onto the beach. And then when the tide goes back out, and takes all the extra water with it, it leaves all kinds of shells and tiny ocean creatures that have washed up from the sea. I have a collection of shells and sand dollars."

"Sand dollars?" she asked.

"Sand dollars are little flat circular urchins with a star pattern in the middle. They live on the bottom of the sea and the tide washes them ashore. Of course they're dead then, and can't bite," he teased. "Seriously, they look like they're made out of the same thing shells are. They don't look like they were ever alive."

"And you collect these things and put them in your house?"

"Sure. Next time I go home I'll get you one."

"Oh, thanks, I'd love that. I want to see the ocean some-day." Mandie's blue eyes twinkled.

"You and your parents will have to come to visit us. I'll show you the beaches and the whole town. Charleston has lots of historical places to see, you know."

"Yes, I've read about it. I'd love to visit sometime."

Mandie became aware that April continually stared at Tommy and paid little attention to her escort. April leaned toward them to hear their conversation.

Seeing some seats vacated near Celia, Mandie stood up quickly. "My friend is at the other end of the porch, and I see two empty seats," she said.

As they walked away, April kept her eyes on Tommy. Even after they had sat down, she was still staring at them.

The maids came out and served tea while Miss Prudence and Miss Hope watched the girls.

Mandie was so nervous she was afraid she would drop something. She looked around to see what the others were doing. Most of them seemed to know exactly how to behave at afternoon tea.

Celia's hand shook so much that she didn't dare lift the cup to her lips for fear of spilling the tea.

Robert noticed that she was not drinking it. "Is some-thing wrong with your tea?" he asked.

Celia blushed and said the first thing she could think of. "Oh, no, I—uh—just don't like tea."

"Well, don't drink it then," Robert said.

"Celia, you should try," Mandie urged. "Miss Prudence might notice that you didn't drink it."

Robert reached over and quickly exchanged cups with Celia. He had already finished his tea. "Here, I'll drink it for you. Then you'll have an empty cup," Robert said with a laugh.

"Thanks," Celia said. "Here comes Miss Prudence now. I hope she didn't see what we just did."

"She didn't," Mandie assured her. "I was watching. She was walking the other way when you swapped cups."

"What if she did see us," said Tommy. "Not everyone likes tea. People shouldn't be forced to drink it just to learn the social graces, as these teachers call it."

Miss Prudence strolled by with Mr. Chadwick and surveyed the various students.

Tommy waited until they had passed, then said, "You know our school is coming over for the dinner party next weekend. Mandie, would you consider being my partner?"

"Aren't we drawing names again?" Mandie asked.

"No, I don't think so. That was just for this first visit. After this we're supposed to know everyone," said Tommy.

"How can they suppose such a thing?" Robert asked. "I certainly don't know everyone." He smiled at Celia. "But then I don't want to know everyone. Celia, will you do me the honor of being my partner?"

"Well, I—yes, if that's the way we're doing it," Celia answered.

"You didn't answer my question, Mandie," Tommy protested.

"Thank you, Tommy, I'd enjoy being your partner," Mandie responded.

Mr. Chadwick stood in the center of the porch. "All right, gentlemen, it's time for us to go home," he announced. "I hope you remembered to ask a partner for the dinner party next week."

Excited conversation broke out among the students as the boys prepared to depart. After saying good-bye to Robert and Tommy, Mandie and Celia walked down the long hallway.

Suddenly, April rushed up behind them. "Tommy Patton is mine for the party," she told Mandie.

Mandie stopped and stared up at the tall girl. "Just what do you mean by that?" she asked.

"Just what I said. Tommy Patton is my partner for the party."

"What did you do, April? Ask him? I'm afraid he has already asked me."

"I don't care who he asked. He's going to be my partner," April fumed.

"He does have a mind of his own, you know," Mandie said. She flashed an amused look to Celia, who stood by listening. "And he asked *me*, so he is going to be *my* partner."

"Let me tell you one thing," April growled at her. "You'd better forget that he asked you, or I'll just conveniently remember that I caught you coming up the backstairs last night after ten o'clock."

"Oh, mind your own business," Mandie said angrily.

April hurried on down the hallway. "I'm warning you," she called back over her shoulder. Then she ran upstairs.

Mandie and Celia just stood there, puzzled by the girl's behavior.

"Well!" Mandie said. "What do you suppose that was all about?"

Celia shrugged her shoulders, and the two girls returned to their room for a rest period before the evening meal. As soon as they opened the door, Mandie noticed that her nightgown was missing. She knew that she had laid it across the foot of the bed. Celia's was there but Mandie's was not.

"It looks like someone took my nightgown," Mandie said, glancing about the room. "If they don't quit taking things, I'm going to run out of clothes pretty soon. My shawl this morning and now my nightgown."

"I'll bet it was that April Snow," Celia accused.

"But she was downstairs on the porch with us," Mandie replied.

"Yes, but she came flying up the steps ahead of us after she threatened you in the hall."

"I suppose it's possible, but why would she do that?"

"I don't know. Are you going to report it to Miss Prudence?"

"No. I can't prove anything. I think I'll just do some detective work on my own. Maybe I can find out for sure who's doing this," Mandie said, as she took another nightgown from the bureau drawer.

Mandie certainly didn't want to get the wrong person in trouble. She wasn't certain that April was taking these things. She would just have to watch April carefully from now on. Although Mandie wasn't a tattletale, she also wasn't going to be threatened, nor was she going to put up with her clothes disappearing.

At supper, April didn't say anything to Mandie, and when they were dismissed from the table, she hurried out to the veranda. Mandie and Celia went to their room to write letters.

Long after the ten o'clock bell had rung and the lights were out, Mandie and Celia lay awake. They talked quietly about the disappearance of Mandie's clothes. Suddenly they heard the clanging metal and squeaking boards again. They looked at each other, and their bodies stiffened in fright.

"There's that noise!" Celia whispered.

"It sounds like it's in the attic," Mandie whispered back.

"It does seem close."

Mandie sat up on the side of the bed. "Let's go see what it is," she said in a low voice.

"No!" Celia objected.

"We don't have to let *it* see *us*. We'll just find out what or who is making that noise," Mandie told her. "Come on!" She started for the door.

"Aren't you going to take a light?" Celia asked.

"Here, we can take this one," Mandie said, lighting the lamp by the bed. She picked it up, and Celia joined her near the door.

All of a sudden, the noise stopped. The girls stood still.

"It went away," Celia whispered.

Mandie set the lamp back down and blew out the light. "We should still look out in the hall," she said, opening the door. Celia was right behind her.

As they stepped into the hallway, someone laughed softly and asked, "And where are you young ladies going?"

Mandie instantly recognized April's voice.

"None of your business, April Snow. And what are you doing out in the hall after ten o'clock?" Mandie asked.

"I'd say that's none of *your* business." April sauntered down the hall toward her room and disappeared around the corner.

The two girls looked at each other.

"April must have been making that noise," Celia said in disgust.

"Maybe and maybe not," Mandie replied, "but we'd better wait for another night to investigate the attic. April may be on her way to tell Miss Prudence that she caught us out of our room. Let's go back to bed."

The girls were really puzzled now. Was April making the noises in the attic? Had April taken Mandie's shawl and then her nightgown? April was always making threats but there still wasn't any proof of wrong-doing. They would have to investigate the attic at their first opportunity and see what was really there.

Chapter 5 / Locked Out in the Night

The next morning, when Mandie started to get dressed, she reached for her blue dress which she had hung on the chifferobe door.

"My dress!" She gasped. "It's gone, hanger and all."

Celia turned to look. "Oh, Mandie, you've got to tell Miss Prudence now. Do you want someone to take all your clothes?"

"I don't understand how anyone could come in here while we're asleep and not wake us," Mandie replied. "I'll talk to Uncle Ned about it. He's coming to see me tonight."

"May I go down there with you to meet him?"

"I'll have to ask first," Mandie replied. "You can stay at the window, and I'll signal if he says it's all right." She pulled out a bright red dress from the chifferobe and took a strand of multicolored beads from a little box on the bureau.

"Those beads are beautiful. Where did you get them?" Celia asked.

"Sallie Sweetwater gave them to me before I left. She's my Indian friend. She's also Uncle Ned's granddaughter." Mandie fingered the necklace tenderly. "These beads are very old," she explained. "Sallie's great-grandmother made them. They're one of my most treasured possessions." Mandie reached for her robe. "Well, if I don't get to that bathroom on time, I won't get a bath," she said.

Later, on their way down to breakfast, the girls met April coming up the steps. They all looked at each other, but no one spoke.

As soon as April was out of hearing range, Celia turned to her friend. "There she goes!" Celia accused. "She should be going the same direction we are for breakfast. I think she is the culprit. And I also think you ought to talk to Miss Prudence, or maybe to Miss Hope."

"I suppose I will, as soon as I get a chance."

At the table, Miss Prudence had already returned thanks and was about to ask the girls to be seated when April rushed in and took her place.

Miss Prudence frowned. "April, I will see you in my office as soon as we finish breakfast," she said sternly.

April nodded without saying a word.

After breakfast, as the two girls walked down the hallway, Celia said, "So April is in trouble with Miss Prudence for being late to the table."

"I'd hate to be in her shoes," Mandie replied. She couldn't wait to tell the whole story to Uncle Ned. He would help her know what to do.

That night when the old Indian came, he and Mandie sat on the bench under the magnolia tree. Mandie kept an eye on Celia at the bedroom window.

"Uncle Ned, I have a problem," Mandie began. "You see, there's a girl here, named April Snow. She and I shared a bed in the other bedroom. She got furious with me because I moved into the room with Celia. You know that Celia and I are good friends. But April said I was moving because her mother was a Yankee." Mandie threw her hands up in the air. "I didn't even know about her mother. Yet April has been nasty to me ever since."

"What she do, Papoose?" the old man asked.

"She watches me all the time. When I was going to my room after your last visit, April met me on the steps. She asked me where I'd been. I didn't tell her, of course. Then yesterday the boys from Mr. Chadwick's School came for tea and April decided she liked the boy I was with. Tommy asked me to go to the dinner party Saturday night, but April says she wants him for her partner. She keeps saying things like, 'I'm warning you' and 'You'll be sorry.' "

"All talk? Not do anything to Papoose?"

"I don't know," Mandie said. She told him about the missing clothes. "I'm not sure whether or not she was the one who took them."

"Papoose tell Miss Head Lady?" he asked.

Mandie smiled at his name for Miss Prudence. "I wanted to ask you if I should mention this to Miss Prudence. The Bible tells us to do good for evil, and if someone smites you on one cheek, turn the other. Uncle Ned, do you think that means I shouldn't do anything to cause April trouble?"

"Papoose not make trouble for girl. Good for girl if Papoose go when sun rises and tell Miss Head Lady," said the Indian. "Must not lose fine clothes. Mother of Papoose not like that."

"I guess my mother would be upset to know I had lost those things."

The old man stood up. "Must go now," he said.

Mandie jumped up and looked at the window above. "Uncle Ned, I promised Celia I'd signal to her if she could come down and meet you. Can she, Uncle Ned, please?"

"Make sign quick. Must hurry," he said, looking up.

Mandie waved to Celia and the girl quickly disappeared. In a few minutes she was running toward them across the yard.

"Celia, this is Uncle Ned," Mandie said. "And, Uncle Ned, this is my friend Celia Hamilton."

Celia curtsied briefly. Uncle Ned smiled and put his hand on her auburn curls.

"No, no, Papoose Celia. Not bow down to me. I only old Indian, not Big God. He only one to bow down to."

Both girls smiled.

"They teach us these things here at school," Celia explained. "A lady never shakes hands. She either nods her head or curtsies, and I thought I should curtsy, from all that Mandie has told me about you. I think you are a great man."

"I only old Indian watching over Papoose," Uncle Ned replied. "Must go now. Come next moon." He turned to Mandie. "Papoose not forget. Go see Miss Head Lady when sun rises."

"I will, if you say so," Mandie promised. She pulled him down for a quick kiss on the cheek.

"Go," he told them.

The girls ran across the backyard and stopped to wave as they entered the screened-in back porch. The old man disappeared into the trees.

Mandie grasped the doorknob and pushed, but the door wouldn't open.

"Celia! The door's locked!" she whispered in the darkness.

"Somebody locked us out?" Celia asked.

"They must have. It couldn't have locked by itself. There's a bolt on the door, remember?"

"April was probably watching us!" Celia accused.

"We'll have to find some other way to get inside the house. There's no way to move the bolt from out here."

"Mandie, please do something about April," Celia complained.

"I intend to, first thing in the morning. But right now, let's look around. Maybe we can find a window open or something. We've got to get back in before someone misses us. I'll bet whoever locked us out is waiting to see what we'll do. Let's go."

Celia followed her friend. They walked all the way around the house without finding any way to get in. Finally, they sat down on the back steps.

"It looks like we'll be caught this time. There's no way in," Celia sighed.

"There's a solution to every problem if you think about it long enough," Mandie told her. She propped her elbows on her knees and rested her chin in her hands. *Uncle Ned has already gone*, she thought. *Of course there probably isn't anything he could do to help us anyway.* Mandie didn't have a friend at the school besides Celia. *Oh, yes, I do*, she thought. *Aunt Phoebe! Maybe she is still up. Aunt Phoebe must have a key to the house*, Mandie reasoned. *She's the first one up. She comes to wake us every morning.*

Mandie jumped up. "Celia, what about Aunt Phoebe? She must have some way to get inside the house every morning. Let's see if she'll help us."

"Won't she tell on us?" Celia asked.

"No. Aunt Phoebe is my friend. Come on."

As the girls walked toward the little cottage, they noticed a faint light behind the drawn curtains. Evidently someone was still awake.

When they stepped onto the small front porch in the darkness, they were suddenly startled to find Aunt Phoebe and Uncle Cal sitting in the rockers on the porch.

"My chillun cain't git in de house?" the old woman asked.

Mandie's eyes widened. "How did you know, Aunt Phoebe?" she asked.

"We sits heah. See lots o' things," Aunt Phoebe replied. She rose from the chair and stood in front of her husband. "Cal, gimme de key."

The old man pulled a door key from his pocket and handed it to her. "Jes' be sho' you don't wake dem two wimmen," he warned his wife. "If you does, we git no sleep tonight."

"We knows how to be quiet. My chillun heah too skeerd not to be quiet. Mistuh Injun Man done gone. Dey got no hep 'cept us."

"You saw Uncle Ned?" Mandie gasped.

"We sees, but we not tell. We knows who Mistuh Injun Man be. C'mon," she beckoned. "We'se gotta go to de front do' wid dis key." Aunt Phoebe led the way around the house.

She quietly slipped the key into the front door lock, turned the tumbler, and slowly pushed the door open. Putting her finger over her lips, she motioned for them to be quiet. Aunt Phoebe pushed them inside, closed the door, and locked it behind them.

The girls stealthily made their way up the main stairway in the darkness. They didn't see or hear anyone along the way. And when they finally closed their bedroom door, they both sighed with relief.

"Whew! That was a close call!" Mandie exclaimed.

"Too close, Mandie."

Just then, the clanging, squeaking noise began again in the attic. They looked at each other in silence. Hadn't they had enough adventure for one night?

With sudden decision, Mandie whirled and opened their door. "Quick! Let's see what it is!"

She started up the attic steps in the darkness. Celia followed, too afraid to speak. The noise grew louder. Slowly and carefully, they tiptoed up the steps until they reached the door at the top of the stairs. A small window by the door gave a dim light. They held their breath.

Mandie rested her hand on the doorknob, trying to decide whether or not to open the door. After a few moments, she gently turned the knob and swung the creaking door open. The room was pitch black. Suddenly there was a sound like a hundred rats scampering across the floor.

The girls panicked and flew back down the stairs, not stopping until they were safe in their room.

"Mandie, I'm afraid!" Celia whispered. "Let's put something in front of our door, so if somebody tries to come in, we'll hear them."

"Yes!" Mandie agreed. She looked around.

The room was small. There was a fireplace on one wall. The bed stood against another. A bureau, chifferobe, and two overstuffed chairs occupied most of the remaining space. A floor-length mirror on a gilt stand stood in a corner.

Mandie made her decision quickly. With Celia's help she succeeded in moving both of the heavy chairs in front of the door.

She stood back and surveyed their work. "That ought to discourage anyone from pushing their way in here."

Feeling a little safer, the girls quickly undressed and hopped into bed.

They soon fell asleep, secure in the knowledge that the chairs were guarding their door. But would the chairs keep out someone who really wanted to get in?

Chapter 6 / April's Trouble

Next morning, Mandie swung her feet out of bed, plopped them on the floor and quickly withdrew them. What had she stepped on? Leaning over the edge of the bed for a look, she let out a sharp cry. The precious beads Sallie had given her were all over the floor.

Awakened by the cry, Celia crawled over to see what Mandie was looking at. "Oh, Mandie! What happened?"

Mandie climbed out of bed and stooped to recover the beads that were scattered everywhere. "Somebody broke my beads, the beads that Sallie gave me." Her voice quivered.

Celia bent to help. "Don't cry, Mandie. I'll help you re-string the beads. Let's just be sure we find all of them."

"How could anyone get in here?" Mandie asked, looking toward the door. "The chairs are moved!" she exclaimed. "I see how they did it. We put the chairs on that throw rug. It would slide easily on the hardwood floor. We went to all that trouble for nothing."

When Miss Prudence arrived at the dining room door for breakfast, the two girls were waiting for her.

Mandie spoke quickly. "Miss Prudence, may I see you a minute as soon as we're finished eating?"

The woman looked at her in surprise. "Why, yes, of course,

Amanda. In fact, I was going to ask you and Celia to come to my office anyway."

The girls glanced at each other, sure that the school-mistress knew they had been out of the house the night before. They ate very little. After breakfast, they followed Miss Prudence to her office.

Miss Prudence stood behind her desk and scowled at the two girls sitting before her. She cleared her throat. "I would like to know what you two were doing out of the house after ten o'clock last night," she said, pausing to indicate the seriousness of the matter. "You know you are not supposed to be out of your room, much less prowling around the yard. Now, I want an explanation."

Mandie decided she had to tell the truth and face the consequences. "Miss Prudence," she began shakily. "We went outside, and then someone locked the back door so we couldn't get back in."

"And what time was that?" Miss Prudence wouldn't give up easily. "Were you outside before or after ten o'clock?" she probed.

Celia tried to help. "Miss Prudence, we—"

Suddenly Aunt Phoebe appeared in the doorway, smiling at the girls. "Miz Prudence," she interrupted, "dese heah chillun come to see me last night, and somebody lock dat back do'." Aunt Phoebe fiddled with her apron. "It was aftuh ten o'clock 'fo' we got Cal roused up and got de key to open de front do'. Dese two was skeerd to death."

The girls couldn't believe their ears.

"Aunt Phoebe, are you telling the truth?" Miss Prudence asked.

"Whut I say is de truth, Miz Prudence. Dey come see me, and somebody lock dat do', and it be aftuh ten o'clock 'fo' we gits dat front do' open."

Mandie realized Aunt Phoebe was telling the truth in a somewhat twisted fashion. For some reason she was trying to keep them out of trouble, but Mandie felt guilty about it.

The old woman stood in the doorway, smiling. She didn't move to go or try to explain why she was there in the first place. She just stood there.

The schoolmistress didn't know what to say.

Then April appeared behind Aunt Phoebe.

Miss Prudence stood up straight and cleared her throat again. "All right, young ladies, I do not believe it's proper to visit Aunt Phoebe so late at night, but go on now to your classes. I do not want to hear of any more doings of this nature." She turned to the Negro woman. "Aunt Phoebe, what did you want?"

The girls got up to leave. Mandie decided not to mention the disappearance of her clothes. She would tell Miss Prudence later when things calmed down. The schoolmistress didn't seem to remember that the girls had asked to talk to her. Mandie and Celia took their time leaving the office, hoping to hear Aunt Phoebe's reply.

"I jes' wanted to know whut you wants from de mahket today," the old woman replied.

"Aunt Phobe, I'll have to see you later about the market," said Miss Prudence. She nodded to the tall girl in the hall. "Come on in, April."

Aunt Phoebe moved quickly down the hallway in the opposite direction from the girls. Then Miss Hope scurried into the office.

Mandie frowned at Celia. "Things are really popping this morning," she said.

"Yes, and Aunt Phoebe sure popped us out of that one," Celia added.

"I wonder why," Mandie said as the girls walked to their classroom.

April sat in Miss Prudence's office, drumming her fingers on the arm of the chair.

Miss Prudence sat behind her desk and Miss Hope dropped into a chair at the side. "April, we asked you to come in here this morning because I wanted Miss Hope to hear what you told me about Amanda and Celia being out late last night." She nodded to her sister. "It seems, however, that it was not their fault. Aunt Phoebe said that they were visiting her before ten o'clock and were locked out. They couldn't get back in until she unlocked the front door. Evidently that was *after* ten o'clock."

Miss Hope leaned forward. "Is that what happened, Sister?"

"Yes," Miss Prudence replied. "Aunt Phoebe stood right there and told me all about it, just now."

"But that isn't so, Miss Prudence," April argued. "I saw them with my own eyes. Mandie went outside first, and then Celia followed in a few minutes. It was after the ten o'clock bell."

"Come now, April, we don't doubt Aunt Phoebe's word," Miss Prudence told her. "You must be mistaken about the time."

"No, ma'am. I was standing by the window in my bedroom, looking out. When I saw Mandie go outside I looked at the clock. It was ten-thirty. In a few minutes Celia followed."

"Then your clock was wrong," Miss Prudence said with finality. "You may go now so you won't be late for your class."

April stood and shrugged her shoulders. "All right. If you don't believe me—" She left the room.

April got as far as the stairway and then turned back, tiptoeing next to the wall. She wanted to eavesdrop on the two schoolmistresses. There was definitely something going on here. She was positive she had seen the two girls go out after ten o'clock, and she intended to hear what the two women had to say about it.

"Sister, do you really believe Aunt Phoebe?" Miss Hope asked.

"Well, I hope she's telling the truth," Miss Prudence replied. "I'd hate to think she was lying for the two girls."

"According to April, Amanda seems to be a born trouble-maker."

"I know her mother is a lady," Miss Prudence mused. "But her father had savage blood. I do hope that wild streak is not going to assert itself in Amanda."

April's ears perked up. She grinned to herself. So Mandie was a half-breed. None of the girls in the school would have anything to do with her if they knew she was part Indian. April would spread the word. This was her chance to get even.

She hurried to her classroom. Since class had already begun, April slipped quietly into a seat near Mandie and watched her.

Mandie always felt uncomfortable when April stared at her. When Miss Cameron asked Mandie a question, she didn't answer.

April leaned over and whispered just loud enough for Mandie to hear. "Hey, half-breed, teacher is asking you a question!"

Mandie's face burned when she realized the girl was talking to her. She crossed her fingers to control her anger.

Looking up at the teacher, she apologized. "I'm sorry, Miss Cameron, I didn't understand the question."

"Please, Amanda, keep your attention on the lesson or you'll never learn anything," the teacher rebuked. "Now I asked you, who became president when Abraham Lincoln was assassinated?"

"Why, the vice-president, Miss Cameron," Mandie said.

All the girls laughed.

"Class, please remember your manners," the teacher scolded, tapping the desk with her pencil. "Now, Amanda, of course the vice-president became president, but what was his name?"

"Oh, Andrew Johnson, ma'am. That was the only way he could ever get to be president." Mandie saw her chance to get back at April for calling her a half-breed. "He was from Tennessee but he was a traitor. I guess the North would take anybody—even a traitor." Mandie hoped April got the slur at her Yankee mother.

She did. In a louder whisper, April repeated her accusation. "I know your father had savage blood."

The girls within hearing distance gasped.

Miss Cameron dismissed the class, and the girls filled the hallway. Mandie waited in the hall for April to come out of the room. She was the last one out.

Forgetting all her resolutions to not argue with April, she walked up to the tall girl, put her hands on her hips, and announced, "My grandmother was a full-blooded Cherokee, and I'm proud of it. I'm part Cherokee because that's the way God made me."

A hushed whisper ran through the crowd.

April turned to the other girls and spoke. "Did you hear what she said? She admits to having Indian blood. What do you think of that?"

Just then Miss Prudence came down the hallway. She couldn't hear the conversation, but April and Mandie seemed to be arguing about something. She walked up and stood between them.

"Into my office, both of you. Immediately!" she commanded.

Everyone gasped and moved away.

But Celia, who had heard everything, came to Mandie's side. "I'll go with you, Mandie," she offered.

"Thank you, Celia, but this is between April and me," she told her friend. Mandie silently followed Miss Prudence and the tall girl to the office.

Taking her place behind her desk, Miss Prudence sighed in exasperation. "Now sit down like two ladies and explain what you were yelling about in the hallway," the schoolmistress demanded.

The girls sat down but neither said a word. April stared at Mandie, hoping to scare her into silence. Mandie didn't want to be a tattletale.

After several minutes Miss Prudence spoke again.

"I asked both of you a question and I expect an answer. What were you yelling about?"

Mandie fidgeted in her chair but did not answer. April kept staring at her, ignoring the question.

"Speak! Now! If I have to call in the girls who overheard this argument, you will both be expelled from school," Miss Prudence warned them.

Mandie was worried. She either had to tattle on April, thereby getting her into trouble, or else not tell and get expelled from school.

Mother would be too hurt, she thought. *I have to explain the situation. I'm sure April won't.*

Mandie sat up straight. "Miss Prudence," she began, "it all started when April called me a half-breed. She said, 'I know your father had savage blood,' and then—" Mandie stopped abruptly.

Miss Prudence's face had turned beet red, and she was gasping for breath. She realized that April had overheard her conversation! Miss Prudence sputtered, trying to think of something to say. She certainly couldn't admit her part in this. Mandie's mother would come to take her daughter home, and the school's reputation would be ruined.

Mandie anxiously leaned forward. "Miss Prudence, are you all right?"

April sat back in her chair, enjoying the scene.

"What? Oh, yes, yes. I'm fine," Miss Prudence replied. She didn't dare look at April.

"Didn't you know that I'm part Cherokee?" Mandie asked.

"Of course I did, Amanda. I knew your father." The schoolmistress regained her composure and then spoke to the other girl. "April, you will apologize to Amanda, and you are immediately suspended from school for ten days. I will send for your mother."

"Send me home if you like, but I will not apologize to Amanda," April sneered. "It's all true. My mother might not even be at home. She was supposed to visit her family in New York after she left me here."

Mandie was sorry that April had to be suspended, but hadn't she brought it upon herself?

"We'll find your mother," Miss Prudence told her. "In the meantime, all your social privileges are cancelled. You will be allowed out of your room only to attend classes and for meals. Remember, you must remain in your room at all other times."

"But the party is tomorrow night," April objected.

Mandie realized how disappointed the girl must be, but she couldn't help feeling some satisfaction that April was being punished.

Miss Prudence stood. "You will not attend the social under any circumstances," she said. "You will be confined to your room." She paused for a moment. "You may go to your classes now. I will let you know when we have contacted your mother, April. And Amanda, I will do my best to restore order after that terribly unfortunate incident," she said.

"Thank you, Miss Prudence," Mandie replied.

At the noon meal the schoolmistress stood before all the girls in the dining room and rang the tinkling silver bell next to her plate.

"Young ladies," she began, "the unladylike conduct of one of our students has come to my attention. I am sure some of you heard April Snow call Amanda Shaw an unladylike name." Miss Prudence cleared her throat and continued. "This is a serious offense, and therefore, April has been suspended for ten days."

The students gasped and loud whispering instantly filled the dining room.

Miss Prudence rang the bell again. "As soon as April's mother can be contacted," she continued, "April will be forced to leave the school for ten days. At the end of that time we will decide whether we would like to have her back. Meanwhile, she is confined to her room except for classes and meals."

All the girls turned to gaze at April, but she didn't seem to notice. April was staring into space, ignoring the whole scene.

Miss Prudence went on. "I want to state here and now that there will be no more of this type of behavior. Everyone is to forget what was said. If I hear of any of you even discussing the matter, you will be liable for suspension, also."

Mandie and Celia looked at each other in shock. Mandie was confused. She felt relief that April was leaving, but she hadn't meant to cause her so much trouble. Still, she did have to tell the truth. There was no way around that.

But now April really had a reason to be angry with Mandie. What if they couldn't reach her mother for a few days? April could have plenty of opportunities to get even.

Chapter 7 / More Noises in the Night

The girls had worked hard decorating the huge barn in the backyard for the party.

They made paper lanterns to hang across the lawn and inside the building. Bright, twisted streamers stretched overhead. Long boards lying across two sawhorses became tables with white bedsheets serving as tablecloths. Dozens of chairs, stored in the loft, were brought down and cleaned. At one end of the barn was a stage used for school plays. For the evening's event, the girls decorated it with magnolia leaves and flowers from the garden. Oil lamps hung in safe places to be lit when needed, and a three-piece minstrel show had been engaged to perform.

Each girl daintily lettered two place cards for the table— one with her name and one for the boy who would be her partner. There were gallons of lemonade in the kitchen and the hand-cranked ice cream churn stood ready. The girls had been helping prepare the food all week. They were even allowed to do a little experimenting. There was more food than they could possibly eat, but anything left would be taken to the local orphanage.

On the evening of the party, Mandie and Celia dressed nervously in their room. Celia wore a pale lavender muslin dress with green lace and ribbons. She arranged her auburn hair in curls and tied them back with a matching green ribbon. Around her neck hung a delicate cameo on a thin gold chain.

Mandie had chosen her pale pink chiffon dress accented with deeper pink rose petals. Her blonde hair hung loosely in ringlets around her shoulders. She wore a tiny silver locket that contained pictures of her father and mother.

Twirling in front of the long mirror in the corner, she laughed. "Hey, is that really Amanda Elizabeth Shaw? I look so old."

Celia came to stand by her. "So do I. I suppose we have to grow up some time, but I don't think I'm going to like it."

"You will by the time you get there," Mandie assured her. "Just think, we won't have to go to school anymore. We can stay home with our families."

"No, you're wrong there," Celia said. "I don't have any brothers and sisters, and neither do you. We'll both be expected to get married and have babies so the family won't run out."

"No, you're the one who's wrong," Mandie replied. "Once we're grown we'll have minds of our own. If we want to get married, we will. And if we don't, we won't."

"I suppose you'll marry that boy Joe you told me about."

"Joe and I—" Suddenly the bell interrupted her reply. "That means it's time for us to go downstairs."

Celia gulped. "Do I have everything on that I'm supposed to? Is it all arranged properly?" she asked.

"You look fine, Celia. Let's go."

By the time all the girls assembled on the veranda, the three surreys full of boys had arrived. Uncle Cal hurried out to help with the rigs and horses.

The schoolmaster left the first surrey and made sure the

boys met their partners in an orderly fashion.

Tommy and Robert immediately spotted Mandie and Celia as they approached the porch steps.

Tommy teasingly bowed to Mandie. "Miss Amanda!"

Robert imitated him. "Miss Celia!" he said.

The girls held back a giggle as they greeted them.

"My, my!" Mandie exclaimed, eyeing their fine dark suits. "You look like real gentlemen tonight."

Tommy pulled at his collar. "These things are terribly uncomfortable," he complained.

"I'm not sure I can eat very much with all this on, either," Robert added. He sat down beside Celia on the veranda.

Celia smiled at him. "I'm not sure I can eat at all."

"Me either," Mandie said. "The girls cooked all the food and it may not be fit to eat."

"We'll manage," Tommy assured her.

Mandie found herself comparing Tommy with her lifetime friend, Joe. Tommy and Joe both had that happy, carefree spirit, but Tommy was taller and looked a little older. She wondered what Joe would look like dressed up in an expensive suit like Tommy's. Joe never wore a suit except to church. And he did wear one to her mother's wedding. But the suits he wore were not finely tailored like these. Still, Joe was her kind of people. And he had told her he wanted to marry her when they grew up.

Miss Prudence cleared her throat loudly. "It is time to go to the barn in the backyard," she announced.

"The barn?" Tommy shrieked. "You mean we're going to have a dinner in a *barn*?" He looked down at his fancy clothes.

Mandie laughed. "It's not what you think," she explained. "The barn isn't used for animals. They've made it into a theater for the school's dramatics class."

As the two girls and their partners entered the building, the boys whistled in appreciation of what they found inside.

"You girls have really been busy," Tommy remarked.

"Thank you for noticing," Mandie said with a giggle. "Now, we're supposed to find our places. We're at the second table next to Celia and Robert."

The four of them walked down the side of the table directly under the loft opening. Celia stopped. "Here are mine and yours, Robert," she said. "Mandie and Tommy are supposed to be next to us."

They all looked, but Mandie's and Tommy's place cards were not there.

Mandie was puzzled. "I know they're supposed to be here. Someone must have switched them."

At that instant, a small piece of straw dropped from the loft above. Mandie looked up. There was a flash of red as someone moved out of sight. April! It had to be! Since she couldn't come to the party because of Mandie, April was determined to make more trouble for her.

Celia saw Mandie looking up. They exchanged knowing glances.

"I think we have an uninvited guest," Mandie whispered to Celia.

By then everyone had found a place and was standing behind a chair waiting to be seated. Mandie and her friends felt embarrassed as Miss Prudence frowned at the four of them standing behind only two chairs.

When the schoolmistress realized what the situation was, she came and asked everyone to move down a little so that two places could be added at the table. While Mandie and Miss Prudence discussed the matter, Robert and Tommy found two chairs across the room and brought them over.

"We'll get to the bottom of this later," Miss Prudence

promised. "I'll have Aunt Phoebe bring more silver and china."

Mandie risked a question. "Miss Prudence, is April Snow in her room?"

The woman looked sharply at Mandie. "She had better be."

"There's someone in the loft," Mandie said quietly without looking up.

"I'll take care of it," Miss Prudence answered. She returned quickly to her place at the head of the table and asked everyone to be seated.

A few minutes later, as Uncle Cal passed by Miss Prudence, she stopped him and spoke to him. The old man glanced upward, then walked to the back of the barn and climbed the ladder to the loft. Mandie watched as he disappeared upstairs. In a moment he came back down the ladder and shook his head at the schoolmistress. Miss Prudence turned her gaze upon Mandie.

Tommy had been watching the whole thing. "What was that all about?" he asked.

"I told Miss Prudence I saw someone in the loft, so I guess she sent Uncle Cal to look. Evidently he didn't find anyone, but there's another way out. There's a ladder at the window on the outside," Mandie told him.

"And how do you know?" he teased.

"Because I've used it," Mandie answered. "We had to take things out of the loft for this party, and I helped."

Tommy grinned at her. "You're quite a girl—or young lady—I guess I'm supposed to say," he corrected himself.

There wasn't a lot of conversation during dinner. The boys were too busy devouring everything in sight. Evidently the girls' cooking experiments were a success.

After the meal, the minstrel show began. The enthusiastic applause was followed by encore after encore. Eventually

Miss Prudence shook her tinkling silver bell and announced that it was time to say good night.

Later in their room, Mandie and Celia chattered about the evening.

Celia plopped down on the bed. "Robert is really nice," she said, beginning to get ready for bed.

"Yes, he is," Mandie agreed, "and so is Tommy. He's going to write me a letter."

"Robert said he wanted to call on me one day soon, but I said I didn't think we were old enough for that."

Mandie nodded and picked up her nightgown. "You're right. Besides, we've got other things to do. We have to learn everything this school wants to teach us so we can get out of here," she said, pulling her nightgown over her head.

Mandie sighed deeply, picked up her Bible from the table by the bed, and sat down. "Tomorrow is Sunday. I need to read my Sunday school lesson before I go to bed," she said. Celia took her Bible and sat on her side of the bed. "We still have ten minutes before we have to put out the light," she replied.

"Our lesson is on the Beatitudes in Matthew," Mandie said. "I sure need to learn all this. It's so hard to love your enemies. I don't think I've been doing a very good job with April."

"Mandie, nobody's perfect. I'm sure God will forgive you for telling Miss Prudence your suspicions about April in the loft. She deserved that."

"But, Celia, it doesn't matter whether or not the other person deserves it. We aren't supposed to do bad things to people when they do bad things to us."

"That's all right up to a certain point. But you had to tell on April. This whole thing is getting out of hand."

"Listen to this," Mandie told her. "Read chapter five, verse forty-four. 'But I say unto you, love your enemies, bless them that curse you, do good to them that hate you, and pray for them which despitefully use you, and persecute you.' " Mandie looked up from reading. "You see, we're even supposed to love people who are mean to us."

"But how can you love someone who acts like April? She's impossible!"

"Celia, I don't know what—" The ten o'clock bell interrupted Mandie's answer. "I guess we'll have to blow out the light, now."

They closed their Bibles, placed them on the table, and Mandie extinguished the lamp.

The girls crawled into bed and were soon dozing.

Suddenly, the clanging, squeaking noise startled them awake. They sat up in bed. The noise overhead sounded even louder this time. Celia grabbed for Mandie in fright.

"Let's go up there," Mandie said. She jumped out of bed. "Only this time we'll take a lamp with us."

"But what if we get caught?"

"Nobody's going to catch us. Come on," Mandie urged. She lit the lamp and picked it up.

Celia stayed close behind Mandie as they tiptoed out to the hallway. Suddenly the house was completely quiet.

"The noise stopped. Let's go back," Celia begged, pulling at Mandie's nightgown.

"No, Celia. We only need one trip up to the attic to see what's making the noise," Mandie said with determination. She started up the dark steps. "I'm going."

Celia gave in and followed. As the two girls approached the attic, they could see that the door at the top of the stairway was closed. Mandie reached forward and pushed the door open slowly. She held the lamp inside the doorway and looked around. The lamp threw only a small amount of light in the dark attic.

Mandie stepped forward. "Look at all the old furniture in here," she whispered. "I don't see a thing that could have been making the noise."

Celia stayed close to her friend. "Let's go, Mandie," she begged. "There's nothing here."

Mandie stumbled over something. The glass chimney on the lamp crashed to the floor. Mandie blew out the light. She couldn't let the flame burn unprotected.

Then, in the darkness, from the other side of the attic, came the clanging metal and the squeaking board noises. The girls turned and ran, stumbling down the dark stairs as fast as they could go. When they reached the last step, they saw a light coming toward them. Before they could find a place to hide, Miss Prudence appeared in her long trailing nightgown at the bottom of the stairway.

She held her lamp up to see the girls' faces. "Aha! So you two *do* prowl around after ten o'clock," she accused. "What have you been doing up in the attic?" Glancing down, she noticed the lamp base in Mandie's hand. "And where is the shade to that lamp?"

Mandie bit her lip. "I'm sorry, Miss Prudence. I broke it. I tripped and it fell off," she explained. "I'll pay for it."

"Yes, you'll pay for it. And you'll also pay for being out of your room. You two will be confined there for ten days except for church, and classes, and meals. And if you don't abide by the rules, it will be much more serious than that. Do you both understand?"

Mandie hung her head. "Yes, ma'am, Miss Prudence," she replied.

"Yes, ma'am," Celia echoed.

"Now, what were you two doing up in that attic at this

time of night?" the schoolmistress demanded.

"We've been hearing noises in the attic," Mandie answered. "And tonight the noises seemed to be louder, so we went to investigate."

"Noises? What kind of noises?"

"It sounds like metal banging, and we could hear boards squeaking like someone walking around up there," Mandie told her.

"Metal banging and someone walking in the attic? How far-fetched can you get?" She turned the girls around and ushered them down the hallway toward their room.

"But, Miss Prudence, we're serious," Mandie protested. "We've been hearing noises like that ever since we came to school."

"We have, Miss Prudence, several times," Celia added.

The woman stopped and looked doubtfully at the two girls. "All right," she conceded. "I'll get Uncle Cal to look in the attic tomorrow. He'll have to go up there anyway to clean up the broken glass. Now, not another word out of either of you." She pointed the girls to their door. "Get in that room and don't come out until breakfast time tomorrow."

The girls quickly obeyed and closed the door behind them. They listened for Miss Prudence to go down the hallway, then began whispering in the darkness of their room.

"What a bad break!" Mandie exclaimed. "If I hadn't broken that lamp shade, we might have found something up there."

"Well, I guess the fun is over." Celia sighed and crawled into bed.

"Oh, no, it isn't." Mandie slipped under the covers on her side. "I still plan to see what's up there."

"Mandie, you don't dare!"

"Oh, yes, I do! And don't tell me you're afraid to go with me."

"But, Mandie, there's no telling what will happen to us if we're caught again."

"We won't be caught again."

"But you always say that," Celia complained.

"Next time we'll be more careful," Mandie promised. "But, Celia, you don't have to go with me if you don't want to."

"No, I don't have to. But I suppose I will," Celia replied. "I just wish I could understand why you're so determined to go up there."

"I can't explain it," Mandie answered, "but something tells me I should keep looking."

"Well, I sure hope it's worth getting into trouble for," Celia said.

Chapter 8 / Caught!

Even though all the girls were required to attend Sunday school and services, they were not all in the same classroom at church. Therefore, Mandie and Celia did not see April until they filed into the pews across the aisle from Mr. Chadwick's boys.

April sat at the end of the pew directly across from Tommy. She tried her best to attract his attention, but Tommy didn't seem to notice her. He looked straight ahead.

Celia poked Mandie and motioned for her to look. Mandie smiled as she and her friend sat down in the pew directly behind April.

During the entire service April kept looking at Tommy. When the audience stood to sing a hymn, she deliberately reached out and dropped her handkerchief in the aisle.

When Tommy didn't respond, she tried other tactics. Quickly replacing her hymn book in the rack, she leaned across the aisle and spoke loudly above the music. "Tommy, do you have an extra hymnal? We seem to be short one over here," she said.

All the girls held their breath and looked to see if Miss Prudence had heard. But the schoolmistress kept singing heartily.

Without missing a note, Tommy handed April his hymnal and turned to share Robert's.

April took the book but did not sing a word. She just stood there holding the open hymnal and watching Tommy. At the end of the song, as everyone sat down, April leaned across the aisle and handed Tommy the hymn book.

"Here, would you put this back where it belongs?" she said loudly.

Everyone nearby turned to look, including Miss Prudence. She frowned at April, then turned her attention to the pastor's sermon.

When the service was over, Miss Prudence guided April out of the church. "This way, April, with the other girls," she said.

The boys left by the other aisle, but April had to go with Miss Prudence. After shaking hands with the pastor at the door, the girls began their short walk back to the school.

Celia nudged Mandie. "Imagine carrying on like that in church," she said softly so no one else could hear.

"I suppose it's her last chance, for a while at least. I heard Miss Prudence tell her that her mother would be here to get her after the noon meal," Mandie said.

"Hallelujah!" Celia laughed.

"Celia, didn't the Sunday school lesson do you any good at all?" Mandie scolded.

"We'll discuss that later."

Mandie sighed. "I guess we'll have plenty of time. Remember, we have to stay in our room except for meals and classes."

"Oh, well, at least that's better than being suspended like April," Celia replied.

Reaching the school, the girls hurried to their room to leave their bonnets, gloves, purses, and Bibles. They would have to move quickly to get to the dining table on time.

As Mandie and Celia entered their room, Mandie immediately sensed something wrong. Looking about, she discovered that her pink chiffon dress was missing. She had hung it on the hook next to Celia's lavender dress the night before.

"Oh, no! Not again!" she exclaimed.

Celia understood immediately. "April!" she accused.

"I'm not sure, but April is going home today. We'll see what happens while she's gone," Mandie said. "Come on. We don't want to be late to the table. We're in enough trouble already."

In the dining room, a tall, arrogant-looking woman stood behind the chair next to Miss Prudence.

The schoolmistress rang her little silver bell. "Young ladies, this is Mrs. Snow, April's mother. April will be going home today, and we are not sure when she will return."

There was no doubt that April went home that afternoon. So when they heard the noises in the attic that evening, they knew it couldn't possibly be April.

Immediately after supper, Mandie and Celia went straight to their room. The sun still shone brightly, and the two girls sat on the window seat, silently watching the other girls stroll around the lawn below.

The noise was barely discernible at first. Gradually it grew louder. The girls looked at each other. A moment later, the noise stopped.

"It can't be April this time," Mandie reasoned.

"No," Celia replied.

"Are we going to see what it is or not?"

"That depends."

"Depends on what?"

"On what you decide," Celia answered. "I always go along with you."

"All right. Let's go." Mandie led the way to the door, and they stopped to listen. "I can't hear anybody in the hall," Mandie whispered. Slowly, she opened the door.

"Quick! Let's get out of this hall!" Celia told her.

They quietly ran for the attic staircase and hurried up the steps. The window let in plenty of light this time, so they could see that the door at the top was closed.

"The door!" Mandie whispered. "I didn't close it last night."

Celia thought for a moment.

"But Miss Prudence was going to send Uncle Cal to clean up the glass, remember? He probably closed it."

"Right," Mandie agreed. She put her finger to her lips, then slowly turned the doorknob and swung the door inward.

The two girls stood at the doorway and looked around. There was enough light to distinguish most of the discarded objects of furniture around the attic: tables, chairs, chests, trunks, and boxes.

"There's nothing here," Celia whispered.

"No, I guess not," Mandie answered. Still looking around, she moved her foot. Crunch. She looked down. The glass chimney she had broken had not been cleaned up. She pointed to it, motioning to Celia.

"Uncle Cal didn't come up here. Who closed the door?" she whispered.

At that moment a huge rat ran across Celia's foot. She screamed. "Let's go!" she cried. Running out of the room, she stumbled down the stairs with Mandie following.

But just as they turned the corner to go to their room, they saw Miss Prudence.

The woman put her hands on her hips and advanced

toward them with a stern expression on her face. "This is it!" she exclaimed. "You have broken my orders to stay in your room. You are both suspended from school for ten days. Celia, I will contact your mother immediately, and Mandie, I will send word for your grandmother to come and get you, since she lives here in town."

Terrible thoughts revolved in Mandie's head. Going to her grandmother's house would be more dreadful than being suspended.

"My grandmother?" she protested. "But, Miss Prudence, I don't really know my grandmother. I don't think she'd want me to come to her house. I've never been there. I've only seen her once in my whole life."

Miss Prudence looked at her in surprise. "And what is wrong between you and your grandmother?" the schoolmistress asked.

"She didn't like my father," Mandie replied, "because he was half Cherokee. She didn't want him to marry her daughter."

"I know all about that," Miss Prudence said with impatience. "But she is your grandmother whether she likes it or not, and she shall hear from me."

Celia hung her head. "My mother is ill, Miss Prudence, because of my father's death. Do I have to go home? It would worry her so much."

Mandie spoke up quickly. "My grandmother's house is huge, so I know she has plenty of room. Couldn't Celia go with me to my grandmother's house?"

"Oh, yes, please, Miss Prudence," Celia begged.

The schoolmistress relaxed her stern expression. "I suppose it doesn't matter where you go, as long as I know you are in responsible hands. But the decision will remain with Mandie's grandmother, of course," she said. "I suppose you girls were in the attic?"

Mandie nodded. "We heard the noise again."

"It certainly is strange that no one else has ever heard these noises," said Miss Prudence.

Mandie swallowed and looked her straight in the eye. "We're not lying about it, Miss Prudence. We really have been hearing noises up there."

"Probably rats. Now get your things together, and do not—I repeat—do not leave that room again tonight. I will send a message to your grandmother as soon as I can find Uncle Cal." Miss Prudence stood watching while Mandie and Celia returned to their room.

The girls began picking up their belongings and piling them on the bed.

"Thank you, Mandie, for asking me to your grandmother's," Celia said.

"Never mind thanking me," Mandie teased. "I'm afraid to face my grandmother alone. But I didn't want your mother to be upset, either. This way, maybe she won't ever find out."

"Then I'm glad I'm going with you."

"Oh, Celia, I just thought of something!" Mandie exclaimed. "Uncle Ned is supposed to visit me tomorrow night. How will he know where I am?"

Celia thought for a moment. "Ask Uncle Cal to watch for him. He and Aunt Phoebe said they saw him when he was here before."

"Smart!" Mandie replied. "I'm glad you're going with me, too."

Later, the two girls stood on the veranda watching, while Uncle Cal loaded their belongings into the surrey.

As they began the drive to her grandmother's house, Mandie spoke her concern to Uncle Cal. "You will watch out for Uncle Ned, won't you, Uncle Cal, and tell him where I am?"

"I sho' will, Missy. I be lookin' fo' 'im," the old Negro assured her. "Phoebe see bettuh in de dahk. I gits huh to watch. Don't you worry none, Missy. We looks fo' 'im."

"I appreciate that, Uncle Cal," Mandie told him. "You know why we're going to my grandmother's house, don't you?"

"Missy, I don' ax. Miz Taft, she tell me y'all gits ten days outa school to spend wid huh."

"Ten days out of school because we've been bad," Mandie said, explaining about the noises in the attic.

"Ain't ne'er been nobody in de attic since years ago, Missy, when I tuck some things up dah fo' Miz Prudence. Ain't nobody e'er goes up dah."

"But we really did hear something—several times," Celia insisted.

"Mought be de rats."

"No, we saw some rats up there, but rats couldn't bang on metal and make the boards squeak, could they?" Mandie asked.

"Reckon not, Missy. Reckon we oughta find out whut's up dah, but I reckon Miz Prudence ain't gonna do it."

"You're right, Uncle Cal," Mandie agreed. "She didn't believe us at all about the noises."

Uncle Cal turned the surrey off onto a driveway leading to a huge mansion.

Celia's eyes grew wide. "Mandie, is this where your grandmother lives?" she asked.

"I'm afraid it is," Mandie replied. "But I've never been inside. My grandmother was never at home when we were in Asheville."

The closer they got, the bigger the mansion looked.

"She sure has a big house!" Celia exclaimed.

Suddenly, Mandie's stomach felt like it was tied in knots.

"Uncle Cal, are you sure she said it was all right for Celia and me to come and stay awhile?"

"Missy, she say, 'You go back right now and git dem girls, tonight. Don't wait 'til tomorruh. Go now.' And dat's whut I done." Uncle Cal stopped the surrey in the driveway near the front door.

A Negro man in butler's uniform appeared at the doorway and came forward, greeting them with a smile. "Evenin', Missy Manda and Missy Celia. Y'all jes' go right in. I bring yo' things."

Mandie and Celia said good-bye to Uncle Cal and walked slowly toward the ornate front door.

At the door, a black maid greeted them. "Evenin', Missies," she said. "Miz Taft, she say 'bring y'all right in.' Dis way, please."

The maid led them down a huge center hallway and through double doors into the most elegant parlor either girl had ever seen. Mandie had thought her Uncle John's house was a mansion, but it couldn't compare with this one. The one time Mandie talked to her grandmother, she had learned that her grandmother was well off. But Mandie hadn't dreamed of anything this beautiful.

Her grandmother sat reading by a window that overlooked a bright, lush flower garden. She put down her book. "Come in, come in," she said, motioning for them to sit in the plush, high-backed chairs near hers. "Sit down. Take off your bonnets and gloves and get comfortable."

The girls sat down, and Mrs. Taft studied Celia carefully.

"So this is Jane's little girl, Celia," she said.

The girls looked at her in surprise.

"You girls don't know it, but, Amanda, your mother went to school with Celia's mother."

The girls turned toward each other and grinned.

"No wonder we're such good friends." Mandie laughed.

"It's almost like we're kinpeople," Celia added.

"I'm so glad to invite you to my home, Celia. I hope you enjoy your stay here," Mrs. Taft said kindly. "Now, they tell me you two kept insisting you heard noises in the attic, and that you kept breaking rules in order to investigate. Is that right?"

Mandie looked down and fidgeted with her gloves. "Yes, ma'am." She lifted her chin. "But we *did* hear noises in the attic. And Miss Prudence wouldn't believe us. So we *did* break the rules, I guess," she admitted.

Mandie's grandmother laughed. "Exactly what I would have done under the circumstances. I have a mischievous streak in me, myself," she said with a twinkle in her eye.

The girls stared at her in amazement.

"Oh, I'm far too old for such tomfoolery now, but when I was young, nothing could have stopped me," she assured them. "You see, Amanda, that is something you have inherited from me."

Mandie smiled. "Yes, Grandmother, I guess we are pretty much alike. I imagine you were a lot of fun when you were my age. And here I was bracing myself for a good scolding from you."

The woman laughed again. "I wouldn't scold you for having a natural curiosity. However, you must remember the old saying: 'Curiosity killed the cat.' "

Mandie sat forward on her chair. "I intend to investigate again when we go back to school," she confided. "That is, if we hear the noises again."

"Oh, no, Mandie," Celia protested. "Next time we'd probably be sent home for good."

"Don't worry about that, Celia," Mrs. Taft said. "They wouldn't dare expel my granddaughter and her friend. That could ruin their reputation in certain circles. I am surprised that Miss Prudence had the audacity to go this far. Actually I rather imagine that she is already regretting her action."

Back at the school office Miss Prudence paced up and down in front of her sister.

"I suppose I shouldn't have been so harsh as to suspend the girls for ten days. I really should have just tried to scare them with the idea. But that Amanda is quite uncontrollable. Rules don't seem to mean a thing to her," Miss Prudence complained.

"But, Sister, Amanda seems to be such a sweet girl," Miss Hope replied. "She was raised in a log cabin, remember? She probably doesn't know any better. I don't think Amanda would deliberately do something wrong."

"But she did. She broke the rules twice, two nights in a row," Miss Prudence reminded her. "I trust Mrs. Taft is not too upset about our sending the girls to her. If she wanted to, she could really make trouble for the school. You know that."

"Yes, Mrs. Taft has a great deal of influence," Miss Hope agreed. "I wouldn't want to get on the wrong side of that lady."

"Well I have decided that when the girls come back to school, I shall try to ignore their curiosity excursions," Miss Prudence declared. "If they want to run around in that spooky attic at all hours, I'll let them—as long as the other girls don't find out."

Miss Hope shuddered. "I can't even imagine having the nerve to prowl around in the attic in the middle of the night," she said. "I wonder if there really is something up there."

That night as Mandie and Celia went to sleep in a huge guest room at Mrs. Taft's, Mandie couldn't get her mind off the noises in the attic. How could she wait ten days to find out what was making those strange sounds?

Chapter 9 / Visitors at Grandmother's House

The next morning, the two girls ate breakfast with Mandie's grandmother in the cheery sun room.

"You young ladies will have to find something to entertain yourselves this evening," Mrs. Taft told them. "I'm sorry, but I had already planned to go to the theater with my friends tonight. I inquired about more tickets, but they are sold out."

"That's all right, Grandmother. We can find lots to do around here," Mandie assured her.

"Lots to do?" her grandmother questioned.

"Yes, ma'am. Like exploring your house. It's fascinating," Mandie replied. Then with a mischievous look in her eye she added, "Or we could investigate the attic."

"I don't think you'll find anything interesting there," her grandmother replied. "I keep my attic clean and orderly, not unkempt like you described Miss Prudence's." She added, smiling, "However, you may give it a try."

The day passed quickly for the girls. They walked around the grounds exploring every nook and cranny. In the stables they found the beautiful thoroughbred horses. They climbed up on an ornate carriage that would be a museum piece someday, and pretended they were grand ladies riding to the theater. Outside, they met Gabriel, the gardener. Gabriel was a tall, stoop-shouldered man who delighted in having a captive audience for a tour of his magnificent gardens.

After a very proper evening meal, Mrs. Taft left for the theater and the girls went to their room. During the afternoon, they had made plans for an exciting night.

"Your grandmother is nice, Mandie," Celia said.

"She seems to be," Mandie replied. "And it was awfully considerate of her to go out and give us time to slip back to school and explore the attic."

Both girls began to change into dark clothes.

"Yes. We'll have to wait until after ten o'clock, but since she said she wouldn't be back till about midnight we've got plenty of time," Celia agreed. She hesitated. "Mandie, do you think we are doing anything wrong?"

"Yes and no," Mandie said thoughtfully. "But I keep feeling that I have to go back. I prayed about it, and I just think I should find out what's going on in that attic."

"Do you really believe God answers prayer?" Celia asked.

"Of course," Mandie replied. "Haven't you ever had your prayers answered?"

"No," Celia answered. "Sometimes I pray and pray, but then I don't know if God answered my prayers or it just happened by itself."

"Oh, Celia, nothing can happen by itself. God makes things happen," Mandie told her. "If something happened after you prayed, God was answering your prayers."

Celia thought about that for a minute. "I wish I had your kind of faith, Mandie," she said.

Before they knew it, the china clock on the mantlepiece was chiming ten times.

Mandie jumped up. "It's ten o'clock!" She grabbed a dark scarf to tie over her blonde hair. Celia did likewise.

Mandie tucked some matches in her pocket. "I just hope

there's a lamp in our bedroom at school that we can use," Mandie said.

"First we have to get inside," Celia reminded her. "They lock all the windows and doors at night, remember?"

"We'll get in somehow. Ready?" Mandie inspected her friend's appearance.

Celia adjusted the scarf over her curls. "Ready," she replied.

Keeping an eye out for the servants, the girls tiptoed down the huge circular staircase and hurried out the front door unnoticed. Earlier, they had unlocked one of the French doors in the downstairs library so they could get back in without alerting anyone.

As they hurried down the dark streets, they saw only an occasional passerby. They went out of their way to avoid the train depot. They knew people might notice them there. A sharp train whistle blew in the distance. It grew louder as a train came into town, and the girls were glad they had stayed away.

When Mandie and Celia reached the school, they began searching for some way to get inside. Cautiously, they pushed and shook various windows and doors, but to no avail. After what seemed like hours, the two were tired and disheartened. They sat down on the back steps to think the matter over.

After a moment Mandie stood and looked up at the second story. "Celia," she whispered. "Look! There's a window up there that's open. I'm pretty sure it's a bathroom."

Celia joined Mandie and looked upward.

"If we could climb up on the porch roof, I think we could get in that window," Mandie said.

"But how are we going to get up there?"

Mandie looked around the walls of the screen porch. She

inspected the posts holding up the roof and the cross boards that supported the screen wire.

"I think we could climb this corner post," Mandie suggested. "See the cross boards there?" Mandie was just about to put her foot up on one of the boards when she heard a low bird whistle. Mandie whirled around. "Uncle Ned!" she whispered to her friend.

Celia followed as Mandie ran around the corner of the house to the magnolia tree where Uncle Ned always waited.

"Oh, Uncle Ned!" she whispered as she took the old man's hand in hers. "I forgot. Did Uncle Cal find you and tell you that we're staying at my grandmother's house?" she asked.

"Cal tell me, but I see Papoose come from road. I wait to see what Papoose do," he told her.

"We're trying to get inside so we can go up to the attic," Mandie said.

"But Papoose already caught for going to attic. Sent away from school. Must not go back inside," the Indian advised.

"But I have to, Uncle Ned. I have to find out what's making that noise in the attic. My grandmother is not home tonight so we came back."

"No, no, no!" the old man admonished her. "Must not do this. Papoose hear train whistle?"

Mandie looked at him, not understanding. "Why, yes, we heard the train coming, but we stayed away from the depot."

"Mother of Papoose and Uncle John on that train. They come see Grandmother," he told her.

Mandie's face lit up. She tugged at his hand. "Come on then. Let's go back to my grandmother's," she said.

"No, cannot go. Next moon will visit Papoose. Go now. You, too, Papoose Celia."

Mandie pulled him down to plant a kiss on his wrinkled cheek. Then grabbing Celia's hand, and holding her skirts high with her other hand, she raced back to her grandmother's house.

Even though they ran every step of the way, when they reached the mansion, four visitors were walking the floor of the library. The maid couldn't find the girls anywhere, and she told them that Mrs. Taft had left Mandie and Celia alone while she went to the theater.

The girls burst into the room through the French doors. There was a big commotion. Mandie spotted Snowball sitting on top of the mahogany desk. She was so glad to see him, she ignored everyone elso, grabbed her white kitten and nearly squeezed the breath out of him.

"Oh, Snowball!" she cried, rubbing his white fur. He purred and licked her face with his little rough tongue.

Suddenly embarrassed that she hadn't spoken to her visitors, Mandie quickly went to her mother and Uncle John. Snowball clung to the shoulder of her dress.

"Oh, this is so nice!" she cried. "Mother! Uncle John!" Tears of joy slid down her cheeks. Then all of a sudden she realized she had two more visitors. She whirled around. "Dr. Woodard! And Joe!" She planted a kiss on the doctor's chubby cheek and grabbed Joe's hand. "It's so wonderful to see all of you."

Mandie then remembered her manners. "Oh, Mother, this is Celia. She's the daughter of your friend, Jane Willis Hamilton."

Elizabeth walked over and put an arm around Celia. "I can't believe it!" she exclaimed. "My daughter making friends with Jane's daughter, and neither one of us knowing it. Celia, I'm so glad to meet you, dear."

Celia smiled. "I can't wait to tell my mother who Mandie is," she said.

When all the introductions were over, everyone sat down and Mandie's mother took on a serious tone. "Now, Mandie, I want you to tell us just where you two have been," she demanded.

Mandie looked at Celia. "We were out taking a walk."

"A walk? At this time of night?" her mother asked.

"Grandmother was gone, and we didn't have anything else to do," Mandie said weakly.

"Amanda, young ladies do not go out this time of night unescorted," her mother scolded.

Mandie stroked her kitten's fur. "I'm sorry, Mother. We won't do it again," she promised.

"You had better not do it again. Something might have happened to you two. What would Celia's mother have thought? Celia's under *my* mother's supervision. Amanda, stop to think once in a while before you do these wild things," Elizabeth lectured.

That completely silenced Mandie. Celia hung her head.

Dr. Woodard tried to lighten the conversation. "We came with your mother and Uncle John to tell you how things are going with the hospital," he said.

Mandie and Celia leaned forward with excitement. Mandie had told Celia how she and her friends had found bags and bags of gold. The gold had belonged to the Cherokees, but Mandie was their heroine, and they put her in charge of it. Now that gold was being used to build a hospital for the Cherokees.

"Oh, please tell us all about it, Dr. Woodard," Mandie said. Snowball snuggled up closer.

"Well, we've got the excavation done and the stakes are up," the doctor said. "It won't take long to lay the foundation and get the walls up. We ought to have it mostly done before cold weather."

Mandie jumped up and danced around the room. She grabbed Joe's hand and pulled him with her. "I'm so glad!" she exclaimed.

Elizabeth watched her daughter, then looked at her husband, and shook her head. Evidently the lessons at the school had had no effect on her.

Joe grasped Mandie's hand tightly to stop her dancing. "We're saving most of the trees," he said. "I told them you didn't want the trees cut down."

"No, don't let them cut down the trees. There wouldn't be any shade, and the birds wouldn't have any place to rest," Mandie said. She walked over to her mother. "When can I go see it, Mother?"

"We need to talk, Amanda," Elizabeth answered. "You and Celia come with me to the parlor." Turning to the others she said, "Excuse us. We'll be right back."

The two girls exchanged glances. Mandie handed Snowball to Joe, and she and Celia followed Elizabeth down the hall. When they reached the parlor, Elizabeth sat on the red velvet sofa while the girls took the chairs.

"Now, young ladies," Elizabeth began, "I want this understood once and for all. If you don't behave yourselves at school, Amanda, you will be brought home to Franklin where I can have you under my own twenty-four-hour watch." And turning to Celia, she said sternly, "Celia, I will talk to your mother, as well. There's no excuse for what you two have been doing. We are sending you to school to learn, not to go traipsing around in dark attics."

The girls' eyes widened.

"Yes, I know about it," Elizabeth continued. "Miss Prudence also sent me word. That's why I'm here tonight."

The girls sat silently.

How can I get her to understand? Mandie wondered.

Something is urging me to keep investigating until I solve the mystery of the noise in the attic. Until I do, I don't think I'll have any peace.

Her mother broke into her thoughts. "As far as your being allowed to see the work on the hospital, that is out of the question right now, Amanda. Until you settle down and apply yourself to your schoolwork, there will be no extra activities. Is that understood?"

Mandie stared at her mother. Elizabeth had never talked to her like that before. *Have I really been so bad that Mother has to lecture me?* Mandie wondered. She blinked repeatedly to keep her blue eyes from filling with tears. It hurt to have her mother scold her so harshly.

Finally, she nodded. "Yes, Mother. I'm sorry," she managed.

Then she really burst into tears and flew into her mother's arms, sobbing uncontrollably. "I'm sorry, I'm sorry," she kept repeating.

Celia silently wiped a tear from her own eyes. Mandie was her dearest friend, and it hurt to see her so distressed.

Elizabeth smoothed her daughter's blonde hair and held her tightly. "All right, Amanda, I love you. That's why I had to make you see the wrong you are doing."

Mandie knew she couldn't make her mother understand how important that noise in the attic had become to her, so she decided not to say any more about it.

Celia finally spoke. "Mrs. Shaw, please don't let my mother know. She's still sick with grief over my father's death. What I have done would hurt her so much. I should have stopped and thought about the consequences before I got into this. I'm more sorry that I can express."

"All right, Celia. I will spare your mother under the circumstances, but remember, this reprimand applies to you, too. You need to settle down and get your mind on your schoolwork," Elizabeth said. "I want you to know I was very sorry to hear about your father. He was a nice man. I knew him years ago."

"You did?" Celia replied.

Elizabeth stood. "Yes, and you look more like him than you do your mother," she said. "Now, both of you go wash your faces, and then come back to the library. I'm sure you'd like to spend some time with Joe, Amanda."

The two girls did as they were told and found a bathroom down the hall. Mandie closed the door behind them. "You know I'd much rather be at home in Franklin than in that silly school. But that's what Mother wants, so I'll try to get through it somehow."

Celia turned on the crystal-handled faucet. "My mother feels the same way, so I suppose I'll have to endure it as well. But it isn't going to be easy." She splashed cold water all over her face, then turned to get a towel.

Mandie looked in the mirror. Her eyes were red and her hair was a mess. She washed her face and tried to smooth her hair.

As they opened the door to return to the library, they heard Mrs. Taft greeting Elizabeth down the hallway.

"What brings you here this time of the night, Elizabeth?" she asked.

"You know what brings me here, Mother. Miss Prudence contacted me."

"You didn't come all the way from Franklin just because Amanda got suspended from school for a few days, did you?"

"Of course, Mother."

Mrs. Taft smiled. "I thought it sounded exciting, poking around in dark old attics, looking for noises." She laughed.

"Mother, it might have been exciting, but it was disgraceful to get suspended from school."

"Oh, come now, Elizabeth. I always wanted you to have that kind of spunk when you were growing up, but you were always meek as a mouse, just like your father."

"Oh, Mother, really!"

"Now, Honey, settle down. Who came with you?" she asked, changing the subject.

"They're all in the library. John is here, and Dr. Woodard and Joe, and Snowball."

"That cat? You brought him on the train?" Mrs. Taft's laughter floated down the hallway.

The two girls slowly made their way back to the library. They both knew it would be fun having Mandie's grandmother on their side. Mandie had prayed so often for her grandmother to like her. Now, for the first time, she was beginning to feel like a granddaughter.

Chapter 10 / Snowball Disappears

After breakfast the next morning, Celia decided to let Mandie have some time alone with Joe.

"If you don't mind, Mandie, I think I'd better wash my hair this morning," she told her friends. "It'll take a while to get dry."

"Oh, sure, Celia. Go ahead," Mandie replied. "We'll catch up with you later."

Mandie led Joe outside. "Let's go to the garden," she suggested. "I want you to see my grandmother's beautiful flowers. And her gardener, Gabriel, is absolutely unbelievable!"

Clutching Snowball, Mandie walked with Joe down the pathway through the flowers, smelling, touching, and admiring. Then they came to a bench by a water fountain.

"Would you like to sit down a minute, Mandie?" Joe asked.

"Sure, Joe," Mandie replied. She sat on the bench and Joe joined her. Snowball curled up on her lap. "Isn't it beautiful here?" Mandie asked.

"Yeh, but I'd much rather be back home. I don't like so much finery."

"Neither do I," Mandie admitted. "I admire this place, but

I wouldn't want to live here. I'll be glad when I get through with that silly school and can go home." She stroked Snowball thoughtfully. "You know Celia and I got suspended for ten days, don't you?"

"Yeh, I know. That was a dumb thing to do."

"I suppose it was dumb, but there's something compelling about that noise in the attic. I feel I just have to find out what it is before it's too late."

"Too late for what?" Joe asked.

"I don't even know," Mandie answered.

"Well, why can't you do it and get it over with, instead of getting caught every time?"

"That's what I intend to do. As soon as I get back to school I'm going to find out once and for all what that noise is."

"Didn't you promise your mother you'd behave at school and not go chasing that noise anymore?"

"No, she didn't ask me to promise. She just said if I didn't settle down and study, she'd bring me home where she could watch me. I didn't make any promises."

"But, Mandie, that was understood. Your mother took it for granted that you had promised."

"I'll try real hard not to get caught again."

"Mandie, that's not being honest. I don't understand what's come over you." He looked closely at her. "You and Celia weren't out just taking a walk last night, either, were you?"

Mandie's cheeks felt suddenly warm. Joe had caught her in a lie.

"We really did take a walk—all the way back to school. We were going to try to get in and search the attic, but Uncle Ned was waiting. It was his night to visit me. And he told us y'all were here."

"Mandie! You had better straighten up and start telling people the whole truth. And you've got to learn something at that school."

Mandie frowned at him. Her face flushed at the tone of his voice.

"You've got to learn something at school," he repeated, " 'cause I don't want a dumb wife," he teased, taking her hand in his.

Mandie's heart beat a little faster. She would never forget the first time he told her he wanted to marry her when they grew up. She took a deep breath. "All right, I'll try to do better. But I do have to find out what's in the attic."

"All right," Joe said, "but hurry up and get it over with. Remember, you can't have everything just the way you want it. Life isn't like that. There's good and there's bad. And there are some things that we think are unbearable."

"I know I have to get an education," Mandie conceded.

"I'm sure your mother would rather have you at home with her every day," Joe reasoned. "But she knows you have to be educated, so she is willing to give you up for a while. Have you ever stopped to think about that, Mandie?"

"I've thought about it," Mandie answered. "But I haven't talked to her about it."

"Well, maybe you should," Joe suggested, and then added, "End of lecture. Now, let's find that gardener you were talking about." He stood up and Mandie followed him. Snowball jumped to the ground.

That evening Mandie talked to her mother as they sat on the sun porch.

"Mother, I have to ask you to forgive me," Mandie began.

"Oh?" her mother replied.

"I'm afraid I told you a lie last night," Mandie confessed. "Celia and I weren't just out for a walk. That was only part of it. We walked back to school to try to get inside and go up to the attic."

Elizabeth studied her daughter for a minute before speaking. "That's what I thought," she said. "I was waiting to see if you would tell me the truth. I knew you wouldn't just take a walk that time of the night."

"I'm sorry, Mother. Please forgive me," Mandie pleaded.

Elizabeth drew a deep breath. "You are forgiven this time but, Amanda, please don't let it happen again. I am not trying to be unkind. I want you to know that I'm only interested in your well-being," she assured her daughter. "Above all, however, please don't ever lie to me again. Whatever you do or get into, I'd rather be told the truth. You should trust me enough to know you can tell me anything. Real love depends on trust." Her voice quivered slightly. "Oh, Amanda, you just can't imagine how much I love you."

Mandie slipped out of her chair and sat next to her mother on the settee. She took her mother's hand in hers and squeezed it hard. "And I love you more than I can ever tell you, Mother. I thank God every day for bringing us together."

After a few minutes of silence Elizabeth wiped a tear from the corner of her eye. "We have to go home tomorrow, Amanda," she said. "Dr. Woodard has patients to see, and your Uncle John has business to look after. I want to leave with the assurance that you will do your very best at school. I shouldn't have to worry about what you might be doing while we are separated."

"I'll learn everything I can," the girl promised. "But, Mother, what good will it do me to learn all those social things? I need to learn more mathematics so I can keep track of the Cherokees' gold."

Elizabeth laughed. "That's what we've got your Uncle John doing. He knows all about money. That's a man's work."

"But, Mother, the Cherokees put the gold in my hands to use for them, and I'd like to keep up with it."

"Don't worry about that. Your Uncle John will sit down with you when you come home and go over every penny."

"And when am I coming home?"

"We'll come and get you for Thanksgiving week. Your Uncle John was planning to keep it a secret, but we're going to visit your Cherokee kinpeople that week."

"Oh, Mother! Thank you!" Mandie hugged her. She couldn't wait to see all her father's relatives at Bird-town and Deep Creek.

"You won't let your Uncle John know that I told you?"

"No, Mother, I won't. Thank you for sharing the secret," Mandie said with a twinkle in her eye. "Since you know Celia's mother, do you think we could invite them to our house for Thanksgiving?"

"We'll decide that later. It would be better if you don't ask Celia until we're sure what plans your Uncle John has for that week."

That night Mandie slept better, knowing that she would be able to see her Cherokee kinpeople at Thanksgiving.

The next day when everyone prepared to go to the train station, they couldn't find Snowball. He had been around Mandie's feet all morning, but at the last minute the kitten disappeared. It was as though he knew they were going to take him away from Mandie.

Mrs. Taft had told the girls that when they returned to school, they could plan to visit her on weekends. So Mandie secretly hoped they wouldn't find Snowball before they had to leave. Then she would be able to see her kitten every weekend.

Finally, they had to quit looking for Snowball. They didn't want to miss their train. At the depot when everyone kissed and waved good-bye, Mandie didn't even shed a tear. She knew she would soon be going home to visit.

Just before Joe boarded the train, he squeezed Mandie's hand.

She whispered in his ear. "Don't let anyone know I told you, but I'm coming home for a whole week at Thanksgiving."

A big smile broke across Joe's face. "I'm glad, Mandie. I really do miss you. Please don't get into any more trouble."

Mandie smiled back at him. "I'll do my best not to."

Later, when Mandie, Celia, and Mrs. Taft returned home, Snowball sat on the front porch waiting for them.

Mandie picked him up and stroked his fur. "You're a smart kitten!" she laughed.

Mandie and Celia enjoyed playing with Snowball during the rest of their stay at Mrs. Taft's. It hadn't turned out to be so bad after all.

The day the girls returned to school, they were packed and dressed, waiting in the parlor for Mrs. Taft to join them. She was going with them to have a little talk with Miss Prudence, she said.

Uncle Cal came from the school to pick them up. After loading their belongings, he waited in the surrey outside.

Snowball rubbed around Mandie's ankles as the girls waited impatiently for Mrs. Taft. They were excited about going back to school. Mandie picked up her kitten and gave him stern instructions. "Snowball, you be a good kitten for Grandmother, and I'll see you soon," she said, smoothing the fur on his head.

The kitten purred in response.

"Come, Amanda and Celia," Mrs. Taft called from the doorway. "We're ready."

Mandie put Snowball down. She and Celia quickly joined

her grandmother in the hallway, then walked out to the waiting surrey. As Celia closed the front door behind them, she didn't notice the white flash of fur darting outside.

When the surrey arrived at the school, Miss Prudence welcomed them. "Please come in," she said, leading the way into the house. She called over her shoulder to Uncle Cal, "You know where to take their things—to their old room."

Mrs. Taft stopped Uncle Cal and said, "When you finish unloading, would you wait for me, please? I will only be a few minutes, but I need a ride back home."

"Yessum, I sho' will," Uncle Cal replied with a smile.

The schoolmistress led them into the little alcove where she had taken them on Mandie's first day at school. The girls sat down with the two women.

"Miss Heathwood, I have come to say a few things that I think ought to be made clear," Mrs. Taft said emphatically.

Miss Prudence glanced nervously at the girls. "Maybe the young ladies would like to go on up to their room," she suggested.

Mrs. Taft raised a gloved hand. "No, Miss Heathwood, I want them to hear what I have to say. I think it is very possible that the school made a serious mistake in suspending these two girls. They are now ten days behind their classmates in their studies because of a silly rule. And I don't think it would be to the school's advantage to engage in such punishment again."

The girls looked at each other in astonishment.

Miss Prudence straightened her skirts. The worry lines in her face deepened. "That's what I was expecting from you," she said. "However, the girl's mother put her in this school, and she is the one who should consult me. Not you." She paused for a moment, then continued. "I'm very sorry they are behind with their schoolwork, but it's their own fault. I must have my rules obeyed, no matter who is breaking them."

Mrs. Taft stood to her feet. "We'll see about that!" she exclaimed. "I'd say you'd better remember who your patrons are." She turned to Mandie and Celia. "Study hard and catch up, girls, and I'll see you next Sunday for dinner."

"Good-bye, Grandmother, and thank you for everything." Mandie almost felt like giving her a hug, but she didn't know how her grandmother would react.

"Thank you for letting me stay in your beautiful home, Mrs. Taft," Celia said.

"You're both welcome," Mandie's grandmother replied. "Now go up to your room and get on with your lessons." In a moment she was gone.

Mandie and Celia stood in the hallway, staring after her.

Miss Prudence came up behind them. "Get your things unpacked, young ladies, and be in the dining room in time for dinner," she said. Without saying anything more, she walked away.

Mandie took a deep breath. "Well, I guess that's that," she said.

"Let's go," Celia urged.

As they unpacked in their room, Mandie bent down to push an extra box under the bed. "I can't imagine why Grandmother did that," she said. Then she did a double take. What was that white thing she saw under there? *Oh, no. It couldn't be*, she thought. Lying on her stomach, she gave it a pull. Out came a ruffled, protesting Snowball. The girls burst into laughter.

"Snowball, how could you do this? You're going to get us into more trouble!" she giggled. "I know Miss Prudence won't allow you here." Mandie shook the kitten gently and looked into his blue eyes. He tried to lick her fingers.

Celia sat down on the floor, rolling with laughter. "He

must have hidden in our baggage," she said.

"Maybe we can hide him here in the room. Then on Sunday we could take him back to Grandmother's," Mandie said.

That plan only lasted part of the day. When the girls left the room to go down to supper that night, Snowball made a beeline through the open doorway and disappeared down the hall toward the main staircase. The girls ran after him, but they couldn't find him.

"I guess we'd better forget about Snowball until after we eat," Mandie said. "If we're late for dinner, we'll really be in trouble."

"We can come back up and look for him as soon as Miss Prudence dismisses us," Celia suggested.

In the dining room the girls looked to see if April Snow had returned, but her place was vacant.

After supper, some of the girls who had never been friendly before, welcomed Mandie and Celia back. The pair must have seemed abrupt in their conversations, but they were anxious to hunt for the kitten.

When Mandie and Celia reached the upstairs hallway they ran into Aunt Phoebe.

"Lawsy mercy, Missies! Y'all sho' in a hurry," the old woman said. "I put food for dat white cat in yo' room."

Mandie looked puzzled. "Aunt Phoebe, how did you know about my kitten?"

"Cal, he say cat sittin' theah 'tween boxes when he unload de surrey. He know cat belong to Missy, so he tuk it up wid de rest, an' shut him up in de room. I lef' milk and food fo' de cat."

"But he isn't in our room. When we came out for supper, he ran out and disappeared," Mandie told her.

"Den we hafta hunt him. Miz Prudence she kill dat cat if she find him in dis house."

They searched everywhere but still couldn't find Snowball.

Mandie and Celia went to their room. It looked as though the kitten had really disappeared this time.

"Let's leave the door open just a crack in case he comes back this way. Maybe he'll come in," Mandie said.

But at that moment, Snowball had plans of his own. He wasn't about to give up the nice lap he was curled up in, or the soft hand rubbing his fur. He was completely happy.

Chapter 11 / The Mystery Solved

Even though Snowball hadn't been found by bedtime, the girls had to close their door. Mandie knelt by the bed to say her nightly prayers.

"Dear Lord, please send Snowball back to me," she prayed aloud through her tears. "I love him, and I don't want anything to happen to him," she said, raising her face toward the ceiling. "I thank you for your help, dear Lord. Amen."

Celia joined her. "Yes, dear God, please send Snowball back to Mandie. He's such a good little kitten. Please send him back," she prayed.

Instead of getting into bed, the girls put out the lamp and went to sit in the window seat. Even after the ten o'clock bell rang, they still sat there.

"You know, in a way I'm glad to be back at school," Mandie told her friend. "I want the time to hurry up and pass. At Thanksgiving, my mother is coming to take me home for a whole week!"

"You're going home for Thanksgiving?" Celia was surprised.

"Aren't you going home then, too?"

"I don't know. My mother hasn't said anything about it in her letters," Celia replied.

"Don't forget to write and tell her that my mother went to school with her. And be sure and ask her if you're going home for Thanksgiving week."

"All right," Celia agreed. "I'll write her a letter tomorrow."

Suddenly they heard the noise. The metal clanged and the boards squeaked. Both girls jumped up.

"Now!" Mandie exclaimed. She reached for their new lamp and the matches. Quickly lighting the lamp, she rushed to the door. Celia stayed right behind her. The noise continued as they cautiously climbed the stairway to the attic.

At the top of the steps, Mandie held the lamp in one hand, slowly turned the doorknob with the other, and pushed the door open.

This time the lamplight illuminated an unbelievable sight. A young girl with big brown eyes and long, tangled brown hair, and wearing Mandie's pink chiffon dress, was sitting on the floor with an iron poker in her hand. She was hammering at the lock on an old trunk.

When the girl saw Mandie and Celia, she froze in fear. Dropping the poker, she backed into a corner. And as the poker hit the floor, Snowball came bounding out of the darkness. Mandie quickly handed the lamp to Celia and picked up the kitten.

For a few minutes all three girls stood there, silently eyeing each other.

Then Mandie stepped forward in anger. "Why are you wearing my dress?" she asked.

The girl merely whined and cowered in the corner.

"I suppose you took my other dress, and my shawl, and my nightgown and broke my beads, too, didn't you?" Mandie accused. "What are you doing up here, anyway? You don't go to this school."

The girl did not speak but watched them fearfully.

All of a sudden Mandie realized that the girl looked sick and hungry. She felt sorry for her. "Are you hungry?" Mandie asked.

The girl still would not speak. Mandie turned to Celia. "Come on. We can get the food Aunt Phoebe left for Snowball and bring it up here. I think she looks hungry."

They hurried back down the steps with Snowball and gave him the bowl of milk Aunt Phoebe had left. Then they took the plate with a piece of meat on it back up to the attic.

When they returned the girl was still in the corner. Mandie advanced toward her and held out the plate of meat. The girl looked at it, then at them, then grabbed the meat from the plate and devoured it. Mandie and Celia watched in amazement.

The poor girl must be starved, Mandie thought. "Do you want to come down to our room with us?" she asked.

The girl ignored the question and kept eating.

"What do we do now?" Celia asked.

"I don't know," said Mandie. "Let's go downstairs and talk. Maybe we can figure out something." She waved to the girl. "We have to go now, but we'll be back," she promised.

When they got to their room, they sat down on the window seat again, and Snowball jumped up between them.

Suddenly Celia gasped. "God answered our prayers," she said. "He sent Snowball back to you!"

Mandie hugged her kitten and looked up at the dark sky outside.

"Thank you, dear God. Thank you," she whispered.

"That poor girl up there!" Celia exclaimed. "There's something wrong with her."

"I wonder why she won't talk," Mandie said. "Who is she? And how did she get up there in the first place? I'd also like to know what's in that trunk she's trying to open. Might be something real interesting. But that will just have to wait."

"Mandie, we've got to tell someone about her," Celia reminded her friend.

Mandie stood up and paced the floor. "I know we can't let her stay up there and starve. But if we bring her downstairs, then Miss Prudence will know we've broken the school rules again. This time she might dismiss us for good."

"But we can't leave her up there like that just to save our own skins. I really think she's sick, don't you, Mandie?"

"I'll send for Dr. Woodard. He'll know what's wrong with her," Mandie said.

"Too bad we didn't find her that night we came over here from your grandmother's. Dr. Woodard was already in town then."

"I know," Mandie agreed. "And now if we ask him to come, then everyone will know everything."

Mandie continued to argue with herself. "But why should she suffer for our sins? We would get into trouble, but she needs help." Mandie paused to think. "Oh, I have an idea! I'll ask Aunt Phoebe if the girl can stay in her house until Dr. Woodard can get here and see what's wrong with her."

"Aunt Phoebe might not agree to that. She might get into trouble, too."

"If I know Aunt Phoebe, she just might be willing to help." Mandie's eyes sparkled. "I'll ask her first thing in the morning."

At five-thirty the next morning, the girls shut Snowball in their room and made their way downstairs. Unbolting the back door, they went outside and hurried across the yard to the little cottage.

Aunt Phoebe, already up and dressed, came to the door. "Lawsy mercy, Missies! What y'all doin' up and dressed dis early in de mawnin'? Git in dis heah house 'fo' Miz Prudence sees y'all." She swung the door open and pulled them inside.

"Aunt Phoebe, we've got a problem," Mandie began, and then explained about the girl in the attic and their idea of bringing her to Aunt Phoebe's house.

"There's something wrong with her," Celia said. "She won't talk."

Aunt Phoebe put her hands on her hips and tapped her foot. "Y'all's a-fixin' to git yo'selves in mo' trouble," she said.

"We thought of that, Aunt Phoebe, but our troubles are not important compared to that girl's. She needs help," Mandie pleaded. "Please, Aunt Phoebe. We'll get her over here without anyone seeing her. No one will know about it."

"And tell me whut gonna happen if Miz Prudence find out 'bout dis?"

"I don't know, but we have to help the girl, even though it may cause trouble for us. We can't just ignore her," Mandie told the woman.

"She's almost starved to death," Celia said with concern.

Aunt Phoebe wasn't convinced. "Best y'all jes' march right up to dat Miz Prudence and tells huh. Let huh take care o' things."

"There's no telling what Miss Prudence might do," Mandie argued. "But if you'll let her stay here until Dr. Woodard comes, he can take her to the hospital or see that she gets medical attention. Please, Aunt Phoebe."

At that moment a loud voice called from the next room. "Phoebe, you do whut dem girls want. I send a message today to dat doctuh," Uncle Cal told her as he came into the room.

Phoebe turned to grin at her husband. "Lawsy mercy, Cal. Dat whut you want done? Heah I'se 'fraid to take de girl fo' fear you don't like it," she said.

"Now you knows we gotta hep Miz Lizbeth's girl," he told her.

The girls smiled broadly.

"Best y'all gits huh right now 'fo' anybody gits up!"

Mandie and Celia ran back to the house and hurried up to the attic. The girl was asleep on a pile of old quilts in a corner. Mandie noticed her other missing clothes lying on the floor nearby. Mandie touched the girl on the shoulder, and she sat up with a start. She stared at them in fear.

"Come on, we're going to eat," Mandie told her.

The girl stood up quickly and backed away.

"We're going to get food," Celia said.

But the girl refused to come near them.

"I have an idea," Mandie suggested. "She likes my clothes. I'll go get a dress and offer it to her."

Mandie and Celia ran downstairs to their room, and Mandie pulled a bright red gingham dress from the hanger. Being careful not to let Snowball out, they rushed back upstairs.

Mandie approached the girl, holding out the red dress in front of her.

The girl's eyes lit up. She advanced toward Mandie with her hand out to grab the dress. Mandie kept moving backward just out of the girl's reach, and the girl followed. They managed to get her all the way down the attic stairs, down the servants' steps, and out into the backyard.

Then Mandie ran ahead waving the dress at the girl. "Hurry!" she called.

The girl followed Mandie right through the front door of Aunt Phoebe's house.

Once inside the house, Mandie handed her the dress and pulled her gently into a rocking chair. The girl rubbed the folds of the dress and made little moaning noises as she rocked back and forth.

Aunt Phoebe studied the girl carefully. "I say she look sick. Sick in de haid," the old woman said. "Now, how do we keep huh in dis house?"

"When you and Uncle Cal leave," Mandie suggested, "just lock the outside doors so she can't get out. I'll bring her some pretty ribbons and things that will keep her entertained until Dr. Woodard can get here," she said.

Uncle Cal put his hands on his wife's shoulders. "Best we feeds huh fust. She sho' look mighty hungry," he said.

Aunt Phoebe pulled a little table near the rocking chair. "I don't know how you gits dat kind of sick people to eat, but I'll try."

She went into her kitchen and after a few minutes returned with a bowl of hot mush and a glass of milk. She set them in front of the girl.

Immediately the girl grabbed the bowl and started eating. But the whole time she was eating, her keen brown eyes watched everyone else in the room.

Aunt Phoebe smiled and patted the girl's thin shoulder. The girl looked up at her and smiled faintly. Everyone was delighted with her reaction.

Mandie approached the girl and stooped down in front of her, smiling. "We all really care about you. We want to be your friends. Can you tell me your name?"

The girl smiled back but did not utter a word.

"My name is Mandie. What's your name?" she asked.

The girl's only answer was a big smile.

"I thinks dat girl don't hear a word we'se a-sayin'," Phoebe said.

"You mean you think she's deaf?" Mandie asked.

Aunt Phoebe nodded. "Dat or she don' know how to talk."

Mandie got up and slipped around behind the rocking

chair. Right behind the girl's head she yelled, "Tell me your name!"

The girl jumped out of the chair and whirled to stare at Mandie.

"Oh, I'm sorry!" Mandie cried. "You *can* hear. I didn't mean to scare you. Sit back down and eat."

The girl just stood there, looking at her. Mandie rested her hand on the girl's shoulder to turn her around and gently pushed her back into the chair. Mandie kept smiling at her. Finally the girl smiled back and picked up her spoon to resume eating.

"Den she don' know how to talk," Aunt Phoebe said.

"Maybe she's just scared—afraid to talk to us," Celia suggested. "She might have had some kind of shock before we found her."

"Well, best you girls gits back in dat house 'fo' Miz Prudence git up and see you, or we's all gonna git a shock," Aunt Phoebe warned.

"Will you get a message to Dr. Woodard for me, Uncle Cal?" Mandie asked.

"I sho' will, Missy. Jes' you write it out and I sees it gits to 'im," he promised.

"We have to go to classes today and I may not get a chance to see you. I'll write a note to Dr. Woodard and leave it under my pillow for Aunt Phoebe to bring to you," Mandie told Uncle Cal.

As Mandie and Celia left, they looked back. The girl was eating and not paying attention to anyone else. They shrugged their shoulders and headed for the schoolhouse.

"So far so good," Mandie whispered as they slipped back into their room. She took a piece of paper from her notebook and sat down. "I don't think I'll tell him the whole story. I'm just going to say a friend needs his help real bad, immediately."

A heavy feeling lifted from her shoulders when she signed the note and tucked it into an envelope addressed to the doctor. She slipped it under her pillow.

At last she knew why she was compelled to investigate the attic. She still might get into trouble over it, but she was glad she had persisted. Now maybe she could help.

Mandie paused for a moment to pray that God would heal the girl, making her well, and strong, and happy again.

"Oh, Celia," Mandie said to her friend. "I'm so glad it wasn't April who took my things."

"And *I'm* glad you didn't tell Miss Prudence about it like I kept telling you to do," Celia admitted. "It would have been awful if April had been blamed for something she didn't do. She gets into enough trouble on her own."

Mandie agreed.

Chapter 12 / Grandmother to the Rescue

When Mandie and Celia arrived at their first class, Miss Cameron greeted them at the door. "We're so glad you are back," she said.

The other girls echoed her welcome.

Miss Cameron's eyes sparkled as she tapped her pencil, calling the class to order. "Amanda, while you and Celia were gone, we made plans for our first play," she said. "And the girls voted on the actresses for it. By a two-third's vote you have been selected for the leading role in the play."

Mandie stared at her teacher, completely speechless. How could she get all those votes? She hardly knew anyone except Celia. *How can I act in a play in front of an audience?* she thought. *I've never done anything like that!*

Celia nudged her. "Say something, Mandie. They're waiting."

Mandie rose in a daze and opened her mouth to speak. Nothing came out. She tried again. "Thank you. I appreciate your confidence in me." Her legs melted and she plopped down in her seat.

The class applauded.

Preparation for the play began immediately and took so much time that Mandie had very few opportunities to see the girl in Aunt Phoebe's cottage. Celia visited as often as possible and kept her up-to-date.

The next few days crept by, and Mandie didn't hear anything from Dr. Woodard. She worried that he might not have received her letter. Maybe it got lost, or maybe he was out of town when it came. She knew he traveled a lot.

Aunt Phoebe and Uncle Cal took good care of the girl from the attic. They gave her food and a bed to sleep in, but they kept the doors locked when they were out of the house. The girl seemed content but still did not say a word.

When Mandie learned that the girl loved Snowball, Aunt Phoebe said she could bring him over to the cottage for the girl to play with. Both Snowball and the girl were happy to have someone to play with, and Mandie was relieved that she wouldn't have to worry about getting caught with her kitten at school.

Everything seemed to be going fine. Then one afternoon during rest period, while Mandie and Celia were visiting, Miss Prudence made an unexpected appearance at Aunt Phoebe's house.

"Aunt Phoebe, I was wondering if—" She stopped short. Miss Prudence came into the room and closed the door. "Amanda, Celia, what are you two doing here?" Miss Prudence asked. "And who is that other girl? Where did she get that cat?"

"Miz Prudence, I kin explain," the old woman began.

The girl from the attic sat still, holding Snowball and staring at the schoolmistress.

"I think you had better explain fast, Aunt Phoebe," said Miss Prudence.

Mandie and Celia stepped forward.

"Blame it all on us, Miss Prudence," Mandie said. "Aunt Phoebe had nothing to do with it."

"Just what are you talking about, Amanda? Blame what on you? Speak up, young lady."

"Do you remember the noises we told you we heard in the attic? That girl was responsible. We found her last Monday when we came back to school," Mandie explained.

"That's right," Celia said. "When we heard the noises again, we went up to the attic and found this girl pounding on a metal trunk with an old fire poker."

Miss Prudence's mouth dropped open. "You found this girl in my attic?" She gestured toward the silent girl.

"Yes, ma'am, and she had been up there at least since school started," Mandie replied.

"Now, how could she survive up there that long?"

Aunt Phoebe spoke up. "I done been missin' vittles from de kitchen, most ev'ry day, Miz Prudence," she confessed. "But I figures some of yo' schoolgirls was a-doin' it, so I ain't said nothin'."

"You should have reported that to me immediately, Aunt Phoebe."

"Miss Prudence," Celia added, "the girl also kept coming down and taking Mandie's clothes. She was wearing one of Mandie's dresses when we found her."

Miss Prudence drew a sharp breath. "This girl has been stealing clothes, also? We *must* contact the authorities. Find Uncle Cal and ask him to see me immediately, Aunt Phoebe." The schoolmistress turned to leave.

"Wait, Miss Prudence," Mandie said. "You don't understand. There's something wrong with this girl. She can't talk. At least she hasn't said a word since we found her. We can't turn her over to the law."

Miss Prudence whirled in anger. "Oh yes we can, young lady. What else do you think we can do with her?"

Mandie thought quickly. "Send word to my grandmother," she blurted out. "I'm sure she'll take care of the girl until we can find out who she is."

Miss Prudence trembled. She could never let Mrs. Taft come meddling in school affairs again! "Your grandmother has nothing to do with this, Amanda," the schoolmistress said sternly. "This is a matter for the authorities. Aunt Phoebe, I shall be waiting for Uncle Cal in my office, and you young ladies will both report to me after supper. You realize you have broken rules again."

Miss Prudence closed the door loudly.

"So we're in trouble again," groaned Celia.

Mandie had a sudden idea. "Aunt Phoebe, do you know where Uncle Cal is?" she asked.

"He be down in de flow'r garden wid dat man whut tends to 'em. I guess I'd best be gittin' him."

"Wait, Aunt Phoebe. Would you give me five minutes?" Mandie asked. "I want to find Uncle Cal first, and then you can come look for him."

"Lawsy mercy, Missy, whut you be up to now?"

"Just give me five minutes head start and then you can look for Uncle Cal. All right?"

Mandie didn't wait for an answer. She ran every step of the way down the long slope to the flower garden at the bottom of the hill. She arrived out of breath and tried to explain to Uncle Cal what was going on.

Uncle Cal looked worried. "Dat Miz Prudence, she say fo' me to come see huh?"

"Yes, Uncle Cal. Only I have another idea," Mandie said, beginning to breathe more easily. "Would you please rush over to my grandmother's first? Tell her about our finding the girl in the attic and everything. And ask her to come, just making a call," Mandie directed. "If she acts like she knows about the situation, Miss Prudence will suspect you told her. I don't know what Grandmother can do, but I'm sure she'll do something."

Uncle Cal went along with Mandie's plan. When he told Mrs. Taft the whole story, she immediately ordered her buggy brought to the front door. After arranging for someone to give Uncle Cal a ride back to the school, she climbed into the buggy and headed out. Driving herself, she took the long way around, stopping by the newspaper office. There, she talked to the publisher, Mr. Weston, and his photographer, Mr. Hanback. When they heard the story, they hurried to the livery stables to get their horses.

Next, Mrs. Taft dropped by her pastor's house and persuaded him to meet her at the school. Then when she told the story to the mayor, Mr. Hodges, he promised to arrive soon after she did.

Mandie's grandmother smiled to herself as she urged her horse on. She hadn't had this much fun in years. In a short time, Miss Prudence would have more than she could handle.

Arriving in front of the school, Mrs. Taft tied the reins to the hitching post and hurried inside. She found Miss Prudence in her office, waiting for Uncle Cal.

Miss Prudence looked up in surprise. "Good afternoon, Mrs. Taft," she said. "Do come in."

"Thank you," Mrs. Taft replied. She sat down. "Today is Friday and I thought I'd arrive early and see if Amanda and Celia could come home with me now for the weekend, instead of waiting for Sunday dinner."

"Why, yes, I suppose they could," the schoolmistress managed. She was sure Mrs. Taft had come to start trouble. "I don't believe they have any classes this afternoon. However, Amanda is rehearsing for the play."

Mrs. Taft stood. "She can make up for that later," she

120

said. "Do you have any idea where the girls are?"

"Oh." Miss Prudence hesitated. "I'll send for them."

Suddenly Uncle Cal appeared in the doorway. "Missy Manda and Missy Celia be out at my house with Phoebe," he announced. "Dey say you wants to see me, Miz Prudence."

"So the girls are at your house, Uncle Cal," Mrs. Taft said. "I will go and get them." She started out to the hallway.

Miss Prudence hurried after her. "I'll send for them, Mrs. Taft. Please sit down and rest."

"Thank you, Miss Prudence, but I'd like to visit with Aunt Phoebe for a moment anyway," she replied. She continued down the hall and through the doorway into the kitchen.

Miss Prudence thrust an envelope into Uncle Cal's hand. "Take this note to Sheriff Jones," she ordered. "Quickly, Uncle Cal!"

Uncle Cal smiled to himself and obeyed, while Miss Prudence scurried after Mandie's grandmother.

When Mandie and Celia saw Mrs. Taft, they burst into laughter. "Oh, Grandmother!" Mandie cried. "I just knew you'd come."

"So you two finally found the noise," Mrs. Taft said. She looked at the youngster in the rocker.

The girl stopped rocking and stared at her.

"I've got help coming," Mandie's grandmother assured them.

Aunt Phoebe threw up her hands. "Lawsy mercy, Miz Taft, I guess we all be in trouble," she said.

"Don't you worry, Aunt Phoebe. Just leave everything to me," Mrs. Taft replied.

Suddenly there was a knock at the door and Miss Prudence hurried into the room. "Amanda, your grandmother has come to take you and Celia home with her for the weekend," Miss Prudence announced. "You may get your belongings together—whatever you need for the weekend."

Mrs. Taft faced the schoolmistress. "Mandie and Celia tell me they found this poor girl in your attic. Did you not know she was there?"

"Of course not, Mrs. Taft. I had no idea."

"Who is she? What are you going to do about her?" Mrs. Taft asked.

"Evidently she can't talk. They say she hasn't spoken a word since they found her," said Miss Prudence defensively. "I don't know who she is. I'm going to turn her over to the authorities."

"To the authorities? Do you know what they will do with her? They'll throw her in one of those dirty old cells until they can find out who she is. Surely you don't wish that on this poor child," Mrs. Taft argued.

"That is precisely what I plan to do," Miss Prudence replied. "I have already sent for the sheriff."

There was another knock at the door. Aunt Phoebe opened it to find the newspaper publisher, his photographer, and the mayor standing there.

Miss Prudence drew in a sharp breath as she recognized the three men. "Good afternoon, Mr. Weston, Mr. Hanback, Mr. Hodges," she greeted them. "Shall we go to my office?"

The three men pushed their way into the room so they could see the girl.

"No, thank you, Miss Heathwood," said Mayor Hodges. "We didn't come to see you. We came to see this girl who was found in your attic. And we want to talk to the young ladies who found her," the mayor explained.

Before Miss Prudence could ask how they knew about it, Reverend Tallant came through the open door.

"Good afternoon, ma'am," the minister greeted her. "I've

come to see the little girl who was found in your attic."

Miss Prudence caught her breath sharply.

The four men crowded around the girl who had not moved since Mrs. Taft entered the room. Snowball still snuggled in the girl's arms.

Mandie, Celia and Aunt Phoebe stood to one side while Mrs. Taft spoke to the preacher. "How are you, Reverend Tallant? They say the girl hasn't spoken a word since they found her. Maybe you could get her to talk."

He nodded, pulled up a footstool, and sat down in front of the girl. "We're your friends, young lady," he said gently. "How about telling us your name. Can you do that for us?"

Everyone watched in silence. The girl moved her eyes but did not open her mouth.

Just then Sheriff Jones strode into the small living room and walked straight to Miss Prudence, his hat in his hand. "Afternoon, ma'am. Now, where's this girl you want us to take in?" he asked.

Miss Prudence froze as she felt everyone's eyes on her.

The sheriff pulled a note from his pocket. "Your man came by and gave me this note to come over here right away to take in a strange girl," he explained. "Where's the girl, ma'am?"

Reverend Tallant rose to face Miss Prudence. "You sent for the sheriff to come and lock up this little innocent girl?"

Mayor Hodges frowned. "Do you intend to throw this little girl in jail?" he asked.

"What for?" asked Mr. Weston, the publisher.

Miss Prudence took a deep breath. "It's all a mistake," she managed.

Mr. Weston wasn't satisfied. "These two young ladies *did* find this poor girl hiding in your attic, didn't they?" he probed.

When Miss Prudence didn't answer, Mr. Weston turned to Mandie and Celia.

"Yes, sir," they said in unison.

"Tell us all about it," Mr. Weston urged.

"Well, it was like this." Mandie related the whole story, including the two girls' ten-day suspension.

Miss Prudence ended Mandie's story. "And since you young ladies have again broken my rules, the consequences will be much greater this time."

At that moment Uncle Cal pushed his way through the crowd. "Stan' back, please," he announced. "De doctuh man be heah to see de girl."

Everyone moved back as Dr. Woodard and Joe nudged through.

Mandie ran to the doctor. "Oh, Dr. Woodard, I knew you'd come. Please do something. This girl is sick, and we don't think she can talk," Mandie said.

"I know. Uncle Cal told me about it when we caught up with him down the road. I've been away and just got your note yesterday," the doctor explained. "I had to come to Asheville today anyway, so Joe came with me." The doctor glanced at the girl in the rocking chair and then around the room. "Uncle Cal, do you have a bedroom where I can examine the girl?"

Uncle Cal nodded. Mandie tried to get the girl to go into the bedroom, but she refused to budge from the rocker. The doctor ordered everyone to leave except Aunt Phoebe.

Outside, the photographer set up his equipment by the front door to take pictures for the newspaper. Miss Prudence stood apart from the others who were standing around in small groups, talking.

A few minutes later, Miss Hope joined the crowd outside without her sister noticing.

Joe caught Mandie's hand and pulled her over to one side of the yard. "I'm glad you finally found out what was causing that noise. Who would have thought it was anything like this?" he said.

"I told you, Joe, something just urged me to find out what the noise was, and I'm sure glad I did. The poor girl is not well," Mandie told him. "I hope your father can help her."

Miss Hope came up quietly behind them. "So do we, Amanda," she said gently.

Mandie and Joe whirled around and stared.

"This has all been such a shock to my sister, I don't think she knows how to react."

"I never thought about that," Mandie replied. "I guess this could be bad publicity for the school."

"And I'm sure we are both embarrassed that this poor child was shut away in our attic without our knowledge, but I think my sister feels a greater responsibility." Miss Hope looked at Mandie with pleading eyes. "Oh, Amanda, if you had only come to us when you first suspected something."

"I tried to tell Miss Prudence," Mandie insisted, "but she wouldn't believe me."

"Maybe I could have helped," Miss Hope offered.

Joe squeezed Mandie's hand in support.

Mandie looked down at the ground. "I'm sorry, Miss Hope. I didn't mean to cause trouble. I just had this feeling that I should find out what was making those noises. And something good *did* come from it."

"I know your intentions were good, Amanda, and we are all thankful that the little girl is going to get some help." Miss Hope slipped her arm around Mandie's shoulders. "But you made some poor choices in how to solve the mystery. An adult could have been a great help. What if, instead of finding a frightened little girl, you had found an escaped prisoner hiding in that attic?"

Mandie shivered at the thought. "I see what you mean," Mandie said. "I guess maybe rules are there to protect us."

Miss Hope smiled.

Just then Dr. Woodard came out of the cottage. Several people started to question him, but he held up his hand. "I can't tell you much, except that the girl is badly undernourished," he reported. "She can hear, but I don't know about her speech. With proper diet and medical attention, it is possible that she could start talking."

A murmur went through the crowd.

Miss Prudence stepped forward. "But, doctor, the girl can't stay here," she objected. "If you don't want the sheriff to lock her up, someone will have to take her."

Everyone suddenly became silent.

Dr. Woodard walked over to the schoolmistress and raised his voice so that everyone could hear. "Why can't she stay here?" he asked. "Aunt Phoebe told me she would be glad to help the girl. We'll try to find out who she is, but we certainly can't put her in jail in her condition."

Mr. Weston cleared his throat loudly. "My newspaper is going to run a big story on this. We hope someone will read it and identify the girl," he said. "Would you like me to print a statement that you refused to keep the girl on your prem ises, even though your cook volunteered to care for her in her own house?"

Miss Prudence's lips quivered. "No, Mr. Weston. What I meant was that the girl couldn't stay here in the school with my students," she argued.

Suddenly Miss Hope appeared beside the newspaper publisher. "We *are* concerned about the girl, Mr. Weston," she said calmly. "Aunt Phoebe may certainly care for the child. That would be wonderful. We are quite pleased that she is willing."

"Yessum," Uncle Cal spoke up. "We takes care o' de girl 'til somebody find huh people," he said.

Miss Prudence heaved a sigh of relief and everyone seemed satisfied.

With that settled, Mrs. Taft called to the girls nearby. "Amanda, Celia, bring whatever you need for the weekend out to the buggy. Please hurry. Joe and his father are coming with us."

Mandie turned to Miss Prudence. "Are we still in trouble?" she asked.

The schoolmistress took a deep breath. "It was fortunate that the two of you were able to rescue the girl from the attic," she began. "However, since you have broken school rules, you must pay the penalty. Perhaps we'll take you out of the play as your punishment. Then you and Celia will take the responsibility of helping Aunt Phoebe with the girl."

Mandie swallowed hard. "Yes, ma'am," she replied. She hated losing out on the play, but she would enjoy spending time with the girl.

When the Sunday newspaper came out, it displayed bold headlines: "Unknown Girl Found in School Attic." The front page article related the two girls' part in the discovery and asked that anyone having information about the girl notify the newspaper office.

The following Friday, a poorly-dressed man and woman stopped by the newspaper office.

"We seen your story in the paper about the girl found in the attic," the man said. "We think maybe she's ours. You see, we've got a daughter that ain't all there. We've had to keep her shut up all her life. Somehow, she got out about a month ago, and we ain't seen her since."

Mr. Weston asked them a lot of questions and finally took the couple out to the school. Miss Prudence sent Mandie and Celia to Aunt Phoebe's cottage with them.

When the girl saw the people, she went wild with fright. There was no doubt about it. She knew them, but she was so terrified, she jumped out of the rocking chair, ran into the bedroom, and shut the door. In her haste, she dropped Snowball, and the cat hissed and slapped the man's leg with his outstretched claws. The man tried to kick him, but Mandie snatched Snowball up in her arms.

Mr. Weston frowned at the couple. "Evidently that girl knows y'all but she's afraid of you," he said. "What have you done to her?"

"We ain't done nothin', mister. She's our youngest. The rest of 'em done married and left home. But Hilda there, she ain't jest right, so, like I said, we keep her locked up so she don't run away."

"You mean locked up in a room by herself?" Mr. Weston asked.

"Yep. That's the only way we could keep her at home," the man said with a shrug.

Finally the wife spoke. "We couldn't let our neighbors know what a disgrace the Lord sent down on us. We ain't never lived a bad life, and we don't understand why God give us such a child."

"What's your name, feller?" Mr. Weston asked. "Where are you from?"

"Luke Edney, my wife, Mary. We live on a farm over near Hendersonville," he said.

"Well, your daughter is under a doctor's care right now," Mr. Weston informed them. "I don't think you can take Hilda home with you today. We'll have to see what can be done for her," he said.

A few days later, the whole town of Asheville, and the surrounding countryside, turned out for a parade to escort Hilda to the hospital.

Mr. and Mrs. Edney had been persuaded to commit Hilda to a private sanitarium. There she would receive medical attention, paid for by donations.

Uncle Ned came for the festivities, too, and as soon as Mandie could get a chance to talk to him alone, she confided in him. "I'm still concerned about April," she said. "I'm really glad I never accused her of taking my things, but I have been mean to her," Mandie confessed. "When she comes back to school, I'll ask her to forgive me." She sighed.

"Papoose need ask big people help more," Uncle Ned reprimanded.

"That's what Miss Hope told me," Mandie said. "I guess I did make some bad choices," she admitted, "and I've asked the Lord to forgive me. From now on I intend to stay within the rules and ask for help if there's a problem."

She looked thoughtful for a moment then said, "I might not get to be in the play, but I'm glad Hilda is getting medical help. Maybe someday she'll be normal. I'll pray for her every day, Uncle Ned," Mandie promised.

"Yes, Papoose," the old Indian said with a smile. "We both pray. Big God good."

Mandie smiled. "He sure is, Uncle Ned," she replied. "He sure is."

Then Mandie went to find her friend Celia. Grinning mischievously she said, "Don't you think it's about time we investigate that trunk up in the attic?—After we get permission, of course," she added.

Alarm spread over Celia's face. But then she sighed, "Oh, Mandie, how can I say no?"